NASHVILLE SEAL

A NOVELLA

SHARON HAMILTON

DEDICATION AND AUTHOR'S NOTE

One of the greatest joys of my writing career has been the successful collaboration with my narrator, former Nashville singer/songwriter, and now award-winning actor and narrator/voiceover talent, J.D. Hart. The fun stories of his years as a single CW star, and of those artists he was fortunate to play with and for, have wound their way into this story. Remember, this is a work of fiction, and I create things that never happened, hopefully with enough kernels of truth sprinkled in to make it believable.

But let me be clear, any resemblance to anyone either living or formerly living is purely coincidence, or a form of my own active imagination.

I'd also like to point out that I support two main charities: Navy SEAL/UDT Museum in Ft. Pierce, Florida. Please learn about this wonderful museum, all run by active and former SEALs and their friends and families, and who rely on public support, not that of the U.S. Government.

www.navysealmuseum.org

I also support Wounded Warriors, who tirelessly bring together the warrior as well as the family members who are just learning to deal with their soldier's condition and have nowhere to turn. It is a long path to becoming well, but I've seen first-hand what this organization does for its warriors and the families who love them. Please give what your heart tells you is right. If you cannot give, volunteer at one of the many service centers all over the United States. Get involved. Do something meaningful for someone who gave so much of themselves, to families who have paid the price for your freedom. You'll find a family there unlike any other on the planet.

www.woundedwarriorproject.org

CHAPTER 1

T HE BRIGHT STAGE lights always set Jameson Daniels' nerves on edge, until he began to feel the music in his bones. He covered up his shyness, closing his eyes and falling into the rhythm of his music. Then he felt comfortable enough looking out into the crowd he knew to be mostly women, about twenty deep, standing as close to the stage as his security would allow. Though he wore his Transitions shades, in time his eyes adjusted so he could see their gleaming faces. Flashing cameras still made him jump.

The music playing was always their warmup when he walked out with his guitar, his rum and coke discreetly placed close by. But as he stepped up to the microphone, the band would quit treading water and begin some serious groove on. He preferred the heat level hot to begin with. The slow sexy songs came after he was good and sweaty, his voice becoming raspy. That's what the crowd wanted. He aimed to please.

Playing at Halfway to Heaven was a trophy experience for him, as it was for thousands of other up-and-coming Nashville stars who would sacrifice their right leg to have a gig here. If need be, they'd hobble around on stage, just as the old timers did who now drank too much. Drunk or sober, the audience loved them.

At twenty-five, he was perhaps starting late, and he was new to Nashville. But playing at Halfway to Heaven did two things, in order of importance. First, it gave him the chance to meet up with a producer who might buy his songs, or, better yet, offer him a record deal. Second, as the name implied, his social life and sexual needs were satisfied every night with a hot girl who would boost his confidence and stroke his ego, as well as another very important body part. He thought the venue name was well-chosen.

The bright faces of the lovelies cheered him up just as the band gave him that kick of confidence. He began his theme song.

Bring, bring it on, baby,
The night is still young…

He smiled, seeing his old friend, Thomas Becker, bellying up to the bar and raising his drink to him. Thomas had told him, "Shoot, Jameson, any little lady in the audience who didn't have the idea of going home with you tonight sure had one after hearing that song. That's your fuckin' siren song. '*Come fuck me!*'"

Thomas had been right here, his cowboy boots standing where Jameson's were now. And he'd lived in the limelight, but now he basked in the shadow of Jameson's light. He was Jameson's sometimes warmup act, a friend who didn't want to steal from him, just envied and liked him, and didn't expect a handout. And as fast as Thomas's sunk, Jameson's star was on the rise.

Jameson tipped his hat to Thomas, the gesture returned. Then the girls started to scream, arms in the air, as he continued.

We were made for lovin'
We're gonna have it all.

He didn't look for a single face in particular as the sets played on. The band was having a good night, laughing and improvising with each other. The crowd was especially loud and responsive. He tried to take a short break, and they kept begging him to stay on stage, so he accepted someone's shirt, wiped the sweat from his brow and chest, threw it back, and continued.

His break came twenty minutes late. Back in his dressing room, he set his guitar in the stand, removed his hat, and lifted his rum and coke—already prepared for him—to his forehead, as he sat back and propped up his feet.

Music filtered in through the dressing room door as it opened a crack. She had on impossibly tight jeans and red cowboy boots. Her white shirt was wet, sticking to a noteworthy chest. When she gave him that shy smile, he could see the courage it took to sneak into his dressing room and admired her boldness, but remained seated.

Arlen Strickland, Jameson's head of security, barged into the room behind the little blonde. "Sorry, Jameson. She slipped past me." He had a hand on her forearm as the girl frowned and tented her eyebrows.

"I'm sorry, Mr. Daniels. Just wanted an autograph. That's all." Her big eyes flashed up to him in what he knew to be an obvious lie. It tickled him. He was attracted to ladies on the forward side because it masked some of his own shyness.

"Nah, let her stay. She's not bothering me. Go ahead. I'll bring her out in a bit, Arlen."

Jameson stood, pressing his palm against the door as his guard left the little alcove. He caught her admiring the posters of past concerts and other legendary stars plastered over all the walls. It wasn't a glamorous place, but it held so much history Jameson felt as if the music beat deep within the walls of the place.

At last she was done with her perusal and focused on him.

"Well?" he asked, towering over her and seeing her

shake. She had bucked up her courage and now was considering whether it was a good thing. He always enjoyed playing with them a little, so he didn't speak and let her nervousness take over.

"Oh, gosh. I never thought I could actually sneak into your dressing room. I mean, my friend told me she'd hid out in—I can't remember now who it was. Someone big. And I just thought I'd give it a try."

Jameson didn't care for the comment about "someone big" but let it slide. She was here, and he only had a few minutes.

"So you were in luck. Normally, Arlen doesn't let anyone this close. I guess you were a little too fast for him."

She swallowed hard. Her cheeks blushed, and she was having a hard time looking him in the eyes.

"And what did you come here for, missy?" He held her chin with his thumb and forefinger, raising it up so their eyes could meet. Hers were darting all over the place and then finally landed on his lips. She inhaled, and for a second, he thought she'd back up. He tilted his head to the side. "Hmmm? I'm waiting."

"Could…" She swallowed again, let her eyes close for a second, and then pressed through her comment. "Could you sign my shirt?"

"I'd love to."

"Really?" Her eyes widened.

"Of course. Now, just where do you want me to sign it?"

"Um." She didn't move as his fingers left her chin. "Right here?" She placed her palm over her right breast.

"Right there."

"Yessir, Mr. Daniels."

He growled. "Now that's not a very nice thing to say. You ever hear them announce me as Mr. Daniels? That would be my daddy, if I had one, that is."

He stepped closer, mostly to see if she would shrink away, but she stood firm, which allowed the front of his thighs to touch hers. He enjoyed the heat and the shaking he felt there. "Since I'm gonna kiss a very intimate body part of yours, don't you think you should call me Jameson?"

"Kiss?" Her eyes rounded, but she didn't retreat.

"I always kiss before I give an autograph there. Matter of fact, I insist." He snaked his palm up under her white cotton shirt, laying it flat against her bosom, and then gave it a gentle squeeze. His pants tightened as he savored the feel of her smooth flesh.

Without taking his eyes off her, he continued to massage under her bra until he could pinch her nipple between his thumb and forefinger. She closed her eyes and let her lips part. It was too much of an invitation.

His mouth covered hers as he pinched her again. Her little moan was delicious, so he did it again, harder. His tongue played with hers as he inhaled her, commanded her breathing, and smelled her arousal.

"Nice," he whispered. He tucked his face down, lifted her shirt and bra, leaned over, and placed her nipple between his teeth.

She nearly fell backwards, but he held her steady with his left hand splayed at her waist. As he continued kissing and running his tongue over her nipple, he shifted his palm, pressing lower to draw her body closer to him, her legs on either side of his thigh, and let her rock her sex against him.

"Was this what you had in mind, darlin'?"

"Had hoped..."

But then he was kissing her again, deep. He kissed her neck as she wrapped her legs around him. He hiked her up around his hip line and, after two long steps, pressed her into the loveseat in the corner.

His goal was to jack her up so hot she'd do anything with him tonight after the show. He unbuttoned her jeans, slid them down her hips, then lower, moved her panties aside, and put his forefinger deep inside her. She arched, giving him full access.

"Is this what you came for, baby?"

"Yes," she whispered to a pillow that had fallen against her turned face. "Oh God, I never dreamed..."

Jameson had unbuckled his pants when he heard the knock on the door. He hadn't locked it, so he stood up, swearing under his breath as he adjusted his clothes. He addressed the crack in the door quickly, telling Arlen he'd be right out. His cock had turned to granite, and he'd have to play that way the whole set. It actually was something he didn't mind at all.

She hadn't moved—her eyes still closed, her pants still down about her thighs, showing him the v of her white panties between her legs. "Sorry, darlin', I need to run. You can come by later, if you want."

She scrambled to her feet. "Can I come to your hotel after the show?"

He wanted to hesitate, as if he was considering whether or not it was a wise decision. But he knew all along he'd be letting her in.

"Of course. Besides, I never finished that autograph," he whispered as he kissed her again, then released her.

She fluffed her hair and exited the door.

Jameson combed his hair quickly, patted on a little more aftershave and deodorant, gargled with salt water; then he downed the remainder of his rum and coke. He put his hat on last and looked at himself in the mirror.

What a life he lived. Who wouldn't want to do this every night? It was exciting and fun. Most men would kill to have the lifestyle he had. He felt as if he were King of the Road, Rocket Man in the bedroom, and Elvis on stage every night.

In the hallway, heading toward the stage, he heard

them cheering as his name was announced. With his guitar strapped over his shoulder, he adjusted his pants, then his hat, took a deep breath, and walked out into the lights and the screams of strangers all wanting either his body or his music. He didn't care which one it was, as long as they wanted him. He lived for these times.

If he was lucky, the confidence and power he felt right now would last until morning.

CHAPTER 2

T HE HOTEL ROOMS they booked him in were identi-
cal: a chain that was adequate and clean, but the
kind of place where Jameson could never tell what city he
was staying in. Every lobby and room looked familiar to
him. Even the lingering trace of cigarette smoke that
wasn't supposed to be there had that acrid scent he'd
come to expect.

He flicked on the TV out of habit, volume turned
low, and made himself a drink from the minibar. After
kicking off his boots, he picked up his guitar, sat back on
the king-sized bed, and began to explore a tune he'd had
running around his head all day. It was a new song
forming, new words floating by, making him pick up the
spiral bound book and jot down notes.

He knew he was biding time until the little blonde
from this evening dropped by, so he wasn't surprised
when he heard the soft knock on his door.

It wasn't who he expected. She was tall and curvaceous, but not heavy. Her shiny dark hair hung shoulder length. She was wearing a red leather jacket with fringe up the arms, her arms pressed to her body, sending her chest out farther, as she shivered in the cold hallway.

Jameson's rule was always the same. If they were attractive to him, he'd let them in. If not, he'd make an excuse that he was too tired and take a pass. This one was exceptional and worth standing up the little blonde for.

"Well, come on in." He turned on the charm, used the same words, and stepped aside.

He didn't know why women forever tried to take in the room at a cheap motel, telling themselves lies about their purpose in dropping by. It was always this way with every other strange and exciting liaison he'd had over the past three years. She was no different, pausing in the middle of the room as if taking stock of him. He quickly checked the hallway to see if blondie was on her way and found it empty.

He remembered to put the "do not disturb" sign in the key slot just before he let it slam shut behind him.

She was taking off her jacket, revealing long legs and a fine ass. The view was equally stunning when she turned, her red lips forming a smirk. While looking at his sock-encased feet, she dropped her jacket on the bed. Without saying a word, she began unbuttoning her plaid, red flannel shirt, watching him watching her.

"If it makes a difference to you, my name is

Heather," she sighed, as she licked her forefinger and let it travel between her breasts, burying it under the flannel on her left.

"That's a pretty name for a pretty lady."

Her smile was pleasing, warm and sultry. "Your music makes me want to take my clothes off and get nekked," she drawled. He thought Texas, perhaps.

"I like that, too." He meant it. "What was your favorite song?"

"Other Side of the Mountain." She swayed back and forth, swinging her shoulders as she slowly showed her midriff then her red bra. Soon, she'd removed her shirt and begun sliding her jeans down tanned thighs. Her matching red thong appeared so small compared to the size of her bra on top, which was doing double-time trying to keep her tits from springing loose. Her abdomen was flat and well-toned. As if she were a practiced beauty queen, she walked toward him without an ounce of bashfulness present.

Her fingers unsnapped his shirt as her thighs touched his. She placed a kiss in the middle of his chest, rolled her tongue to his left nipple, laved it with a sharp nibble, and followed up with a kiss. His hands found her soft peach of an ass, so perfectly formed for him.

Her hungry gaze snagged him with her dark eyes. She licked her lips and purred, "I'll bet you hear that all the time, though. You make women want to take their clothes off every day, don't you?"

"Right now, Heather, I don't remember. I like that you're taking yours off. Maybe you could help me with mine?"

"If I did, would you sing to me?"

"No, honey, I don't do that. That's for when I'm on stage."

She had removed his shirt and was working on his belt buckle, then undid the buttons at his fly.

"Couldn't we pretend you're on stage here?" She slid his pants down, allowing a red fingernail to travel up the side of his thigh afterward. He wondered if she was going to laugh at the fact he preferred wearing red, white, and blue boxers, but she merely inserted her delicate fingers inside the front opening and squeezed his cock. "If I was really nice to you?" She dropped to her knees, leaned forward, and put the head of his penis in her mouth and sucked, rolling her tongue over him, as her mouth pulled him deep inside her.

It *was* really nice, as she'd promised, and he sent himself a warning, feeling like he might prematurely burst and come in her mouth, ruining his plans for the evening. "I just sing on stage, darlin', but I'd be happy to sing you something special tomorrow night, if you stop by the show."

"What kind of a woman inspires you to write such a beautiful song? And it's so sad, but I love it," she mumbled, as her tongue played with his tip.

Jameson had had enough. He didn't intend to talk about anything that had to do with him or what made him do things. He wanted to fuck her, had wanted to fuck for the past four hours, ever since the encounter with the little blonde in his dressing room. Now, he regretted not fucking her because he was almost too aroused. If they played much longer, he wouldn't achieve the satisfaction he was seeking, for both of them.

He grabbed a condom he kept in the nightstand, pulled her to the bed, and lay back against the pillows, his erection so thick it was nearly causing him pain.

"Let me," she whispered as he opened the packet. Her fingers smoothed the ribbed plastic over his cock, raising one eyebrow as she did so. "I like the way you prepare."

"Always, darlin'."

He brought her up on top of him, massaging the lips of her sex with his fingers, pulling aside the elastic and sliding her over his hardness until he hooked himself at her opening. Her knees at the sides of his hips, she arched back as she rose up. Then he grabbed her hips and forced her down on him.

Her long sorry moan was achingly sweet, tele-graphing her need and the satisfaction of having him deep inside her. He helped her body move up and down on him, each time arching his own hips to receive the depth of her warm channel. She bounced as he impaled her, her full breasts kissed by warm, pink knotted nipples she squeezed herself.

He could smell her arousal through the sweaty heat they were making, flesh slapping against flesh, as he tried to give her more than she could handle. Yet she wanted more.

He was going to explode when her muscles began a rolling wave, milking his cock. He pressed one thumb down against her clitoris where they were joined, and she unraveled.

He tossed her onto her belly, roughly spread her knees apart, and lapped her juices from behind as she shuddered and convulsed in front of him. Her salty taste nearly had him spilling, so he grabbed a pillow, inserting it under her belly and raising her rump up at the perfect angle, plunged in deep, and held. Catching a breath, he pulled back and then rammed inside again, holding. She melted beneath him, totally conquered, releasing and clamping down on him.

He bit the side of her neck, her shoulder. She dug her nails into his thigh, so he spanked her. Her muffled "Oh" drove him crazy. He reached under and rubbed his forefinger against her nub, causing her to bounce and shudder until he'd wrung her out. His seed flowed, the satisfying release taking him over the threshold into a dream state.

He was lulled to near sleep with the sounds of her heavy breathing. At last, they rolled to the side, and he buried his face in the hair at the back of her neck, and in that perfumed forest, he began to fall asleep. He was fairly sure he'd never slept with her before. He didn't always remember faces, but he remembered bodies. Still, the routine was as familiar as if they'd been partners for years, like a memory was trying to surface he'd long tucked away. Maybe he was remembering the lady from North Carolina who had become the standard bearer for him.

Just before he allowed himself to let go and tumble into the deep satisfying rest he needed, he heard the faint knocking on his hotel room door.

CHAPTER 3

HEATHER WAS A fragrant, fading memory, having left in the early morning hours. He noticed on the way to the elevator that she slipped something on the fourth finger of her left hand when she didn't realize he was looking, just before she safely tucked herself behind the elevator doors.

He figured half the women he slept with were married, about to be married, or about to be divorced. Those ladies were probably a bit safer for him, to be honest. He'd enjoyed himself and hoped she did, too. There wasn't any expectation of a future meeting, and that worked just fine for him.

Early morning was one of his favorite times of the day. Alone at last, naked and satisfied, resting in the sheets with their lingering combined perfume. Sometimes, he'd stay up and write songs or pick on some chords he was working on. His confidence was fired up. He told himself this was a good thing; that he took away as much as he gave in these exciting encounters. There was nothing better than to feel he'd satisfied a woman's fantasies. Nothing better than to be the *object* of her fantasy, even if it was only for one night. Well, sometimes, two or three. Those were some of his best memories.

He remembered that one particular little lady from North Carolina he used to wonder about. It happened when he first came to Nashville. Clean fresh face, pretty smile. Their lovemaking was slow and arduous, and after all these years, he still remembered how she cried when she came beneath him. He didn't want them to cry, but her genuine tears made him feel oddly powerful. Making love to her made him feel healthy. It was nice when that happened, and it wasn't often that way with his girls, not that it wasn't pleasant.

He just never had to go home with some of the girls like his friend, Thomas, did. Jameson attracted the hotties. But Thomas always had a bit of a grey cloud hanging over his head, a little sadness, so his choices were limited. He used to laugh, "Jameson, I'm still going to bed at two with a ten and waking up at ten with a two." It made him smile that even Thomas was able to find someone to spend the night with. It was hard being alone, being on stage every night, and then being alone afterward.

Jameson and the little girl from North Carolina had

spent a whole week together one time when he got booked into one of the gigs in Charlotte—the last time he saw her. She had stayed out of sight in the corner of the front row, didn't seem to mind when other girls threw themselves at him. He had tried not to search for her in the shadows, wondering if she saw what the other ladies were doing. Embarrassing themselves. If she had objected, she didn't say anything about it afterward.

She had even introduced him to her parents, whom he had a hard time facing, but she insisted. They had never talked about getting married, just a few lovely days together. He had peered into her father's eyes and told him, non-verbally, that he wasn't going to do his daughter any harm. He could tell by the way they shook hands that the man believed him. He preferred to think that he'd sent her halfway to heaven during those days. Her parents' horse farm had been a wonderful rendezvous for them when they'd gone to Europe that one spring. The fields of flowers, tasty wine, and picnic baskets full of home-baked goodies were just some of the memories he had. He lived the life most men could only dream of. Did she remember him? He wondered.

Of course she did. They all did. His Facebook page was filled with friend requests, both old friends and friends wanting to be more, and women he'd bedded who were now married or in the process of divorce. He had to be careful accepting some of them. Didn't want to give them the wrong impression. He had to stop accepting the midnight instant messages, too. They stalked him. There were the occasional husbands who asked him to give their wife a thrill they felt they could no longer give. These were good men who had been injured or lacked confidence or just wanted to do something for their wives because they loved them. Jameson understood this, but never agreed. He just couldn't knowingly take what wasn't his to take. And then there was that model from Florida who wanted him to sleep with her fourteen-year-old daughter.

"I know you'll be gentle with her. Make her first time memorable."

There wasn't any kind of money or favor that could make him do that. It had nothing to do with how sweet the little one was, or how scared, or how he knew he could please her, give her something she'd dream about forever. It had to do with his own honor and integrity.

These requests were becoming more urgent and more frequent. That was the part of the fame that was beginning to take its toll.

HE SLEPT IN late, ordering a big breakfast and lots of coffee. He read the paper, listened to a CD a friend had given him, and padded around in the white robe left by the hotel.

He practiced for about an hour, then took a nap, and

woke up in the late afternoon, taking his time to prepare for his show. He returned phone calls and checked his email and Facebook accounts. There was a message from Blondie.

Sorry I missed you. I'd like to be part of your plans for this evening if you're available. No worries, if not. I couldn't stop thinking about you.

She signed her name, *Karen*.

He was happy she didn't show her claws or accuse him of standing her up. It was wise she didn't mention it and let him know her interest was, if anything, stronger. That was always so attractive in a woman.

THE CROWD WAS even larger this evening. One of his band members had been stopped and tagged with a DUI so a newbie base guitarist was brought in. The kid looked hardly eighteen, but he was obviously a virtuoso. Jameson knew that most of the guys in his group were talented enough to go out on their own some day. But for now, they were the club band, working with artists who didn't have their own entourage. They were there to make him look good and make the customers stay longer to buy more drinks.

Making hay while I can.

The music business was fluid. Back-up singers and musicians would one day become huge country stars. It was random and rigged. There were lots of things one had to pay attention to, but the break-out was still sheer luck. Lady Luck was usually on Jameson's side these days, a luscious broad of a gal so generous with her assets and her gifts. So while he was waiting, kneeling at the altar of her fair smile and golden touch, the ride was real fun. Better than he deserved.

He saw Blondie front and center, and when their eyes connected, she made her way back to the bar. Thomas was there on his usual perch. He'd not been Jameson's warm-up tonight because the club owner was trying to promote a new girl group. Sipping on his third drink, or more, he sidled up to Blondie, and Jameson noticed she gave him the cold shoulder.

At the end of the first set before break, he gave the crowd one of the songs they'd come to hear, his new anthem,

Hope you find what you're looking for
Maybe this time you won't come up short...

He studied her swing on the stool, her impossibly long legs and tight blue jeans flaring out at the thighs and hips as she crossed and uncrossed her legs. Her red boots matched her lipstick. She'd gone for a siren look when he preferred the innocence of the night before better, but it didn't matter. She was appearing hotter on the stool as he sang, and that was always a good thing. The more heat she radiated back to Jameson, the drunker Thomas acted. His old musician friend was sitting next to someone he'd never have a shot at in a million years. It was just the luck of his hand. When he was young, he hadn't spent his years wisely. Now that he was older, he couldn't reclaim those days or repurchase his dignity. It was all gone.

Jameson made a mental note to spend some time with his old friend, whose hair was allowed to grow longer and whose eyes were looking wilder.

At the break, Jameson wasn't surprised when Arlen poked his head in.

"You up for the little fan-girl moment, boss?"

"Red boots?"

"Just like you like 'em. Red boots, blonde hair. Nice chest. The works, I'd say." Arlen gave him a wink of admiration. "You certainly know how to get 'em. I think she's the one from last night, but I wasn't lookin'."

Jameson tossed back his drink and set his guitar down, but didn't stand. "Sure you weren't." He winked at his former Marine bodyguard. "Send her in."

She was obviously working hard tonight not to be forgotten. Everything was exaggerated. Her shirt was unbuttoned dangerously deep. Her cheeks blushed bright reddish pink, her lips full and bright red. Even her nail polish was red. She leaned against the dressing room door and looked like the perfect kind of eye candy he needed for the night. He'd be hard again for the entire second set, for the second night in a row.

"Missed you last night, darlin'." It was the right thing to say.

She examined the toe of her right boot and smiled down upon it. "Absence makes the heart grow fonder. You must have needed your beauty sleep."

Sleep was the last thing he'd needed. Right now, he needed to be inside her, but he would wait, *needed* to wait, *and loved* the waiting.

"I agree. So you're Karen?"

"I am."

He stood, holding out his hand for a proper shake. "I'm Jameson. Glad to know you. Hope to know you better later on," he said as they shook hands. He leaned into her frame, still leaning against the door, and gave her a long, languid kiss. She wasn't all over him, which he appreciated. Her lips and tongue and breathing told him what she had in mind, and it was perfect.

"Not gonna let you get me all hot and bothered like last night," she whispered to his ear and then kissed him there. "That was not fair. Not fair at all."

"No, it wasn't. I'm a wicked man." He did believe that statement. Standing her up last night just added to the intensity he was feeling now for the encounter they would have tonight.

"I'm counting on it."

He watched her eyes smile before her lips did. His dick was granite. He widened his stance to give himself room, but she cupped him, with a little squeeze.

"You're still room four-oh-two?"

"Yes, ma'am."

"Thought maybe I had the wrong room. I'll be quicker this time."

A part of him didn't like that comment. Did she know he'd chosen someone else who'd gotten there first? He didn't like being that kind of a man. His ego had made him jump for the first person in line. It worked out this time, but a shadow fell over that decision. He was staring into a mirror and asking a tough question.

"You can take all the time you want, sweetheart. Nice to wait for things, sometimes. Last night, I was just tired." He hated lying. There was shadow number two. What the hell was going on? Bad timing for a sense of conscience.

"Glad you're rested then, cowboy."

She threw her arms up over his shoulders, her soft tits pressing against him so tight he could feel her knotted nipples. She allowed him to move her ass into his groin and nibble at her neck. She smelled delicious. Her flawless white skin tasted as if it was dusted in sugar. He wondered if she tasted that good all over and guessed she did.

BACK OUT ON stage, Jameson watched two suited men standing at the back of the crowd. His opening song was the new ballad he'd written recently and hoped to record, and he directed his attention to them as he sang.

Never knew how much you loved me,
Now it's all gone away…

He threw his heart into the lyrics, with the soft accompaniment of the band behind him. They knew that these were the guys he'd invited to hear him and this was the song he was pitching. Their careful accompaniment didn't interfere with his timing, and like good dancers on a dance floor, they held back some of their own talent to showcase *his* voice and *his* guitar picking, enhancing it without covering it up. They made him sound smooth and practiced, not like the dull pounding ache he felt in his chest or the thick pulsations in his jeans. He was grateful for the end of the song because he was beginning to feel light-headed.

The crowd erupted into raucous applause, but all Jameson saw was the backs of these two men, as they tipped their hats to Karen and a couple of other little ladies at the back, disappearing into the midnight blue smoky air outside of the club. He knew it wasn't their style to run up and give him an enthusiastic handshake and tell him how much they enjoyed the song. They might be on their way to go listen to some other up-and-coming country star, after all. If a week went by and they didn't call, then it wasn't something they wanted. But his gut told him this one could make his break-out. He just didn't care that they'd been so casual about it.

Now that the tryout was over, he threw himself into firing up the band and the audience.

Near the end of his last set, a fight broke out. He watched Arlen get tossed aside and land on his butt, sliding into a table full of young men wearing baseball caps. Arlen stood up, addressed the asshole who'd shoved him, and was once again sent back to the floor like a rag doll. This time, when his bodyguard attempted to stand, the men in caps held him down and backed out of the fray. Two tall guys turned their caps backward and stood up to the troublemaker with their chests extended. The guy was hoisted up by his shirt by one of the men; the other had the back of his pants at the beltline, and together, they ushered him outside with a slight toss at the end.

A woman was ready to go outside and join him, but one of the tall sandy-haired men grabbed her arm and said something in her ear. The group appeared as one unit, a well-oiled cadre of buddies. Jameson thought his bodyguard had shriveled in size, and he was glancing up on stage to see if his boss had noticed.

And I'm gonna love you until the end of time.

The song ended as he added a riff and a "Love you all. Thanks for coming tonight. Let's hear it for Jameson's Band of Brothers. We got Albert Lopez, Little Jimmy here, Virtuoso Kid here who's new tonight, and Cuz Daniels. Thank you, Halfway to Heaven. Y'all have a great evening!"

He wanted to step off the stage and go see the boys who'd helped him out before they left, but did the right thing and exited stage right, leaving the band to tinker, finding out if they were going to be requested for an encore. He always was. Tonight was no exception.

The clapping and cheering subsided and morphed into cheers and whistles as Jameson returned to the stage. He took a long drink of his rum and coke and began the two swan songs. He was tired. What he really wanted to do was go find out what had happened at the back of the club. And then relax with Karen.

He only had about eight minutes to do the first thing and all night to do the second.

CHAPTER 4

LIZZIE CARTER WAS almost toppled by the gentleman being shoved out the door. One of the bulky guys who she knew must be military added his heartfelt apology,

"So sorry, ma'am. Are you hurt?"

She couldn't believe the size of his arms, the tats that were everywhere, the round face with a couple of days of stubble that stubbornly had curled and matched his long hair framing his ears and the back of his shirt. The ends were lighter and curled up, like a swimmer's hair. Then she laid eyes on his startling blue eyes and nearly sent herself backwards, forgetting this evening's mission.

She'd come to see Jameson perform, but seeing this tight package poured into oversized jeans and rolled up sleeves that could barely hold his biceps, almost made her forget herself. Almost, but not really.

"Ma'am?" he asked again, his brows coming together, covering his worry lines.

"No. Sorry. No. He just stepped on my foot, is all."
She glanced down and saw her heel had come out.

"Here, let me take a peek at that. You sit on over
here," the tatted Adonis insisted.

In thirty seconds, she was the object of their attention, the whole table of them. She counted six, and
another two lingering by the doorway, with three more
at a table nearby. They had a collection of a couple dozen
empty beers in the center of the two tables. Someone at
the bar wasn't doing his job, she thought.

With her foot and ankle stretched, draped over the
guy's thigh, he unlaced her shoes and then carefully took
out her foot. She almost heard a collective sigh from the
group.

"Who are you guys?" she asked. None of the men
were paying any attention to Jameson, who had come
back on stage for his encore.

"Concerned citizens," someone in a Puerto Rican
accent added. "Coop here is a medic, and he's examining
your ankle to make sure you don't sue the bar."

"Oh." She was surprised at that comment. "So you
guys are security then?"

That made the whole group of them chuckle. Someone uttered something and was punched in the arm for
his comment. She wished she could have heard it.

"In a manner of speakin', ma'am," answered a handsome African-American man, who had the same baseball

cap the others had, reversed. He flashed her a grin with too many teeth. "Name's Jones, Malcolm Jones. This here is Armando, Jake, Tyler, Luke, T.J., and we got others over there."

"Well, thank you for watching out for me." She angled her head to catch a glimpse at the doorway. "You expecting that guy to come back?"

One of the men was chatting up the woman who had wanted to leave, engaging her in a conversation that made her blush.

"Oh, that's just Alex doing his lady thing. I guess he figures he's got a ghost of a chance since she has such bad taste," Jones continued.

"Bad taste?" Lizzie wasn't sure what he meant.

"Well, we think she came with the dude who's ass...sorry, ma'am...got tossed out of the bar."

As if he'd heard Jones, the man he'd pointed out as Alex raised his beer and offered to bring the dark-haired lady over for a chat. She stiffened and declined, attempting to leave again, and was gently restrained by Alex.

Jones turned around to watch them. "I guess he doesn't think it's a good idea that she follow after that scumbag. Or are they friends of yours?"

"No. I don't know either one of them. But she's wearing a wedding band."

Jones turned around to verify the comment. "That's a fact." He focused back on Lizzie. "Good eyes there, sugar."

She blushed in spite of herself.

"Notice you don't wear one." He raised one eyebrow and leaned back to hear her answer while Coop started to insert her foot back into her running shoes.

"You're fine, I think. Does it hurt at all?" Coop asked her.

"No." She jumped as his delicate fingers cinched up her laces, and he patted her ankle. No one had ever touched her ankle that way before.

Who were these guys?

The music had stopped, so when she heard Jameson's deep buttery voice, the back of her neck became sensitive, the sound of his gentle timbre and cadence sending a delicious electric current down her spine, something she remembered from before.

"You guys show up to my gig to give foot massages now? Did Charlie over there send you guys here to warm up the crowd?" Jameson asked.

Lizzie removed her leg from Coop's thigh and sat up, holding down her hair as if she was wearing a wig. She was still getting used to the new bright red color.

"Just checking her out," said Coop.

"That's what I'm sayin'. You okay, darlin'?" Jameson kneeled down and looked right into her eyes and didn't register any recognition whatsoever. The closeness of his face, the smell of the sweat from his performance, and the beads of moisture on his upper lip were all familiar things. Even the mint on his breath was the same. She'd tasted those mints, had a whole drawer full of them at home, and every time she had one, she remembered how he tasted when he bent to kiss her.

It usually left her vacant and wanting. Tonight, seeing him in the flesh, was no exception.

"I'm fine. Thanks for asking," she answered him. Her voice was a little high and creaky, not her real voice. Her nerves were jumbling her insides.

She'd thought about it every day for the three years plus since she'd last seen Jameson. It had haunted her, how it would be to see him again. To see if he remembered that wonderful week together in North Carolina.

The answer was, painfully, no. He didn't remember her.

A blonde girl she'd met before somewhere came up behind him, placing her palms on his shoulders, and laid claim to him, giving her a smile short on patience.

Jameson rose, adjusted his belt, and slipped his arm around the blonde's waist.

"So you guys wanna tell me what all happened here, since you weren't giving foot massages?" Jameson asked.

"Heard a little domestic squabble," Coop answered. His eyes searched back and forth between Jameson and the blonde. "Maybe he had reason to distrust his wife coming here to see you?" Coop nodded toward the dark-haired beauty at the doorway with Ryan.

Jameson cleared his throat and gave the woman a nod. The lady was smiling devilishly back at him.

"I see what you mean," he answered. But most important to Lizzie was that he didn't deny anything. Jameson began to crane his neck. "Where's my Marine guy?"

Coop and several of the others chuckled.

"What? Did I say something wrong?" he asked, as he pulled the blonde closer to him, massaging the top of her neck while she draped over him like a warm blanket.

"I'm sorry," the handsome Puerto Rican man answered. "That's no Marine or even Marine-in-training."

"Four tours overseas," insisted Jameson.

"I'd say he's had no military training, Mr. Jameson, sir. No offense, but I think you hired what we call a poser." The accented man gave him a lethal wink and then directed it right at Lizzie.

Arlen appeared as if he'd been summoned, introducing himself. A couple of the men asked him questions the bodyguard struggled to answer and was failing miserably. Even Lizzie could see that. The boys didn't call him on it, just let the conversation dangle. Several started to to leave.

"You okay, Red?" one of the men asked, returning his cap to front position, the picture of an elongated skull adorning the front above the bill. She'd seen it somewhere before.

"Hold it," Jameson demanded. "You guys friends of the Punisher?"

"Some of us knew him," the tall medic answered.

"So you're SEALs then. That right?"

The accented man stood and rolled his shoulder. "Could be." Others began to rise and follow his lead.

"What the hell are you doing in Nashville?" asked Jameson.

That seemed to strike a chord with the rest of the boys, several making grunting noises as they laughed.

"We've been on a training mission," said the African-American SEAL.

"The camp. That terrorist camp. You guys did that?"

Several of the young men searched the room. The medic put his finger to his lips. "Jameson, you have yourself a nice night. We'll be on our way."

Jameson unhinged himself from the blonde. "Come by tomorrow. Drinks on me. I'll make sure there's no cover charge. I'd like to talk to you guys. Seriously, you be here tomorrow—I'm buying. Food, too, if you want."

"Sure. We'll see if we can come back. In the meantime, you take care of Arlen here. He's gonna need help standing up and sitting down," laughed another one of the men.

"You coming by tomorrow, Red?" the same young man asked.

She didn't know what else to do, so she nodded.

"Well, that does it for me then. I'll be here," the SEAL answered Jameson, winking at Lizzie.

One by one, each of the men nodded to her, looking her straight in the eyes, not like men who usually hang out in bars. They left the building, leaving Jameson with the blonde, the dark-haired beauty, and herself.

It was an awkward couple of minutes, until Jameson tipped his hat to the lady at the entrance and then slowly to Lizzie herself. He still didn't know that she had dreamed about this meeting for years and that it was over all too soon. Perhaps never to happen again.

Jameson wound his way through the crowd of tables, arm entwined in the blonde's waistband, as the dark-haired girl disappeared in the opposite direction, out into the night air. All that was left was Lizzie's heart beating fiercely in her chest. Everyone was gone, leaving her behind, just like that spring.

Except this time it was happening in Nashville.

CHAPTER 5

KAREN WAS DESERVING of more than he had to give her this evening. His mind was stuck on something about the SEALs who came to watch him perform. He was also stuck on the bad decision he'd made hiring Arlen. Then there was the confrontation with the husband and seeing Heather again.

Just twenty-four hours ago, his world had been so carefree. Now it felt complicated, as if some earthquake had moved all the goalposts.

Karen was a lovely girl, even though she put on the red tonight. She'd be easy to live with, to love.

"Honey, all I got is beer and little bottles from the minibar. You'd probably prefer something else, maybe nice wine or something, and I'm not stocked up. We could go out if you want." His feelings were getting complicated. Was he trying to make up for something he'd felt ashamed of? He'd never had this much doubt before and shrugged it off. Normally he was high as a kite, ready to party to oblivion. The night air was especially cold and threatened rain, and she was shivering.

Is this what I'm doing? Going on a date?

"Are you hungry, Jameson?"

"I could do with some carbs, if you're hungry. I could buy us a nice bottle of something, what? Wine? Just feel bad I don't have anything other than the minibar, and honey, the hotel room is nothing to write home about. Just warning you."

"I wasn't planning on telling a soul." She kissed him, standing on tiptoes. It did cheer him up a little with her happy countenance. "I don't have to work tomorrow morning, so I'm good either way. Up to you. How do you feel?"

He wished he didn't have to be the one to decide all of a sudden.

She agreed to leave her car at the club, and the two of them rode to a little Italian restaurant he'd occasionally visit after a night of partying. The place was beginning to shut down, but the owner knew him and fixed them some pasta and gave them a bottle of house wine. After they ate, he insisted Jameson take the rest of the bottle back home with him.

Inside the hotel room, he left the lights off. It had been a long evening already, and he was starting to get tired. But he owed Karen his full attention, and he was still feeling a twinge of guilt he couldn't shake off. Images of the upset husband kept playing around in his head, sobering his demeanor. He was wondering what was becoming of his usual stellar judgment.

Her angelic hair glowed in the moonlight as she removed her clothes and slipped under the sheets. He was grateful they weren't having the drawn out clothes stripping parade he'd had last night.

Once naked, he covered himself with a condom and found her warm body fully accepting of his. Her legs wrapped around his waist, and he barely had a chance to lean down and plant a kiss on her lips before she'd angled herself on him. He was so damn hard and she was so tight the friction between their bodies quickened the passion he'd been holding back. He stroked her slowly, letting her pull at his butt, bringing him deeper inside with every thrust. Her little mewling sounds were sweet.

"Mmm, those little sounds you make, Karen. Real sexy like."

She giggled, thrusting her pelvis up toward his groin, rocking herself on him. He placed his palms under her rear, holding her up off the bed as he bent one knee, angling to the side and pressing into her to the hilt. Her moans became desperate. She drew her knee up over his right shoulder as he continued his hip-rocking action and then held himself against her insides, pulsing. Her little body shook beneath him as she came, and they shared their pleasure together.

He stroked her hairline with his thumb. "Sorry, darlin'. I guess I was a little tired."

"Oh God, no! Jameson, I can't believe…"

He cut her off with a deep kiss. "Shhh. We're just two people here. Just you and me. I'll make it up to you, sweetheart. Give me a little time."

He rolled on his back, staring at the ceiling he could not see. She fit nicely into the hollow beneath his arm, snuggling her breasts against his, wrapping her legs around his thigh. Her warm, moist pussy pulsed against him. He removed his condom using the top sheet and then reached over to feel the smooth skin of her rump.

"Wake me up if you want to, Jameson, when you're ready."

Well, suddenly, he was ready.

HE WAS GRATEFUL for this life, he thought as he showered with her. Karen's body was perfect for him. He even enjoyed how the hot water made her nipples knot and how her cheeks pinked when he knelt in front of her in the shower and 'tuned her G string,' as he called it.

He bought her breakfast, and then it was time to part. He drove her over to pick up her car at the club. The place was looking dingy and didn't have any of the sparkle of the night before. Nothing had the sparkle of the night before.

What's happening?

He gave her a hug, kissed her on the cheek. She grabbed his ears and planted a deep kiss on him, nearly jumping him again in the parking lot.

"Whoa! Whoa! I need my energy for tonight's show. You forget, I work tonight."

She frowned. "So do I. But I can come tomorrow night."

He smiled into her blue eyes and wanted to be kind, but didn't want her thinking they were going to be exclusive for any length of time. "We had a nice time together, Karen. I think you clear wore me out. Might need a few days to recover."

He saw that the flattering remark appeared to work. But he was serious about her not expecting anything more from him. It seemed a good way to let her down.

Her smile rewarded him with the reassurance his message was delivered. He gave her a good pat on the rear, then a squeeze on that fine ass of hers. "Laters, baby."

She started to walk toward her car, then turned around, her eyes filling out round. "Seriously? You into that, too?"

He placed his fingers on his hips and shook his head, examining the tips of his boots. "Not really. But I saw the movie."

Her warm smile cheered him long after she left,

swaying back and forth in the late morning air, a thing of beauty and something he'd seriously enjoyed. He was also glad it wasn't going to get complicated.

Jameson was surprised to see Thomas's pickup still in the parking lot. It occurred to him the man might have spent the night on a cot in the men's restroom, like he'd done a time or two. The club owner's older light violet Cadillac with the longhorns welded to the grill was also still there.

He found the front door to the club open. Reed, the club owner, was sitting at a table counting money.

"You knocked 'em dead last night, Jameson. You only got two more nights. How about extending a bit for me? The boys said they were available."

"Hell, Reed, they're always available. They work for you, not for me. Besides, I might be a signed recording artist by then. One can never tell."

"Shit, Jameson, you should just enjoy the money and the tits and ass while it lasts. I know Thomas did."

"Well, I'm not Thomas. You should know that by now. He in the bathroom?"

"Shit, no. You should have seen who he went home with last night."

Jameson smiled at the wily manager who continually came out on top. "So you didn't pay him yet; otherwise, he'd have brought an expensive one home. His truck is still here. So where's the asshole holed up this time?"

"No, goddammit, I didn't pay him because I thought maybe that one might steal from him. She rode in on a Harley, and do you see a black Harley outside?"

"I sure don't."

"That's because she took him on *her* bike. The lady, if you can call her that, has more tats than Thomas has. Indian gal nearly three hundred pounds. I can't even imagine the kind of war games she took out on his sorry ass."

They heard the unmistakable sounds of the Harley in question arriving outside the club.

Thomas ran through the opening as they heard the sounds of the bike fade behind him. "Whoo hoo! Now that was some kind of fun! That woman can suck the rockets off a space ship!" Thomas's enthusiasm was double any Jameson had seen in the past several months.

"Glad to hear it," he chuckled as he fist bumped his old friend.

"Reed, can Jameson and I bum a beer? I'm starved."

"You need breakfast, Thomas, not a beer." Reed continued counting without taking his eyes off the money, his lips forming a thin line. "Maybe lover boy can take you out for something. If you come back in an hour, I'll have your money."

"Ah, just one beer, Reed. Come on."

"What are we celebrating?" Reed asked him, stopping to give Thomas attention. "You celebrate gettin' laid now? Is that how it's gone for you, son?"

Jameson could see that cut a little close to the bone for Thomas. "Come on. I'll buy you some breakfast, and we'll pick up a six-pack on the way back."

"Okay." Thomas headed toward the door then turned back to Reed. "See you in an hour or less." After they were in the parking lot, he asked, "So what are you hankering for?"

"I'm not hungry. But I'll get a cup of coffee with you. Tell me about your sexual exploits."

"My lips are sealed, but man, hers? Hers were divine!" Thomas smirked, his eyes wild and twinkling. "Can I ride along?" he asked, pointing to Jameson's truck.

"That bad, huh?"

"Some would call it good, my man."

"So did you stop drinking at all last night?" Jameson smelled the alcohol on Thomas's breath, the clove cigarettes in his clothes.

"I did several things all night long, Jameson. You're not the only stud in Nashville."

"So Reed says she rides a Harley. Most of those girls have boyfriends who don't talk much, but love to pound on white boys any chance they can. You thinking straight?" Jameson squinted, shaking his head. They'd arrived at a twenty-four hour coffee shop.

"Never better."

It was probably a boost to Thomas's ego, plastered and beat down by a long series of rejections from agents and record producers. Jameson knew his old friend had more talent in his little finger than most everyone else in this town. Thomas was also one of the busiest singer-songwriters in Nashville, but only because he was cheap, practically free to hire, and didn't have a personal life. Hanging out in bars for the odd chance of meeting a biker chick, or making enough to satisfy his bar tab, was the trajectory he was on.

"Don't you ever think all this might be ruining your chances of making it big time? You know the A&R guys don't hang out at some of the places you play."

"Well, there were two there last night," Thomas objected. He sat across from Jameson while their waitress, Dottie, came over and placed a couple of sticky menus in front of them.

"Just coffee, please, ma'am."

"Make that two, and I'd like some eggs and toast." Thomas growled, frowning into the menu as she snatched it from his hands.

"Thomas, one guy was there because *I* invited him. He was there to see me."

"Didn't stay very long."

"They never do. I'm feeling good about this one, though."

Thomas nodded, lowering the corners of his lips and

raising his eyebrows. "You wind up with the little high schooler?"

"She's not in high school. She's twenty-two."

"Ah," Thomas said and winked. "Well, shit, I'm happy for you."

"I don't do it for the girls, Thomas."

"Why the hell not?"

"Well, I mean, what kind of a life would that be? I'm working hard to get discovered."

Thomas gave him a glare straight from hell. Dottie brought his eggs and toast just in time. He softened his look after taking his first bite. "I seriously hope it happens for you, man."

Jameson sat back and took stock of his old friend. "You givin' up on the dream, Thomas? Is that what this is all about?"

"You know, for such a smart kid, you sure say the dumbest things." Thomas was pointing his fork at Jameson's nose. "I fuckin' work hard at it every day, same as you. I show up. I play the gigs people like you and old Reed give me. I don't go begging for work. I *find* it. Sometimes I find work that actually pays enough to make my rent. I don't complain. You ever hear me complain?"

"No. I don't. But—"

"Just shut your pie hole." The fork in the air again. "I've never given up any more than you have. But you know as well as I do, your chances in this town are just not very good. We work our butt off. We show up and try not to get too drunk or booed off the stage and try *not* to go home with someone else's wife—" The fork went down, but Thomas leaned into the table and whispered, "Which is more than I can say for another someone in this establishment."

"Didn't know she was married until after."

"Listen to you justify yourself."

"How do you know Tawanda Amazon with the Harley out there isn't married?"

"Because I fuckin' asked her."

"Oh, and you believe her?"

"Did you even ask the lady?"

Jameson said nothing, staring down at his coffee cup.

"No. The answer's no. You just let her into your room when she dropped by; am I right or am I right?"

"Thomas, where is this going? You did the same fuckin' thing fifteen years ago when you first started out. You told me yourself."

Thomas threw his fork down on his now-empty plate, sat back, and showed Jameson both of his palms. "I rest my case."

Jameson was so pissed off he was about to leave and let the old singer walk or take a taxi, except he figured Thomas didn't have money for the taxi and he might get arrested for being drunk in public if the right kind of asshole cop were to find him.

Thomas was really his only friend, or at least the only person in Nashville he could trust with anything other than a bottle. He saw perhaps his own future. Was this where he was headed?

No. I'm special. I have what it takes. I'm not giving up on this dream of becoming a big star. Not everyone makes it. Most don't. But I can do it. Maybe Thomas didn't want it bad enough.

He scanned the lines on his friend's once-handsome face, the well-worn shirt collar he couldn't afford to replace, and the white tee shirt underneath that was starting to turn yellow. He noticed the calluses on the man's fingertips from years of playing, the knuckles that were starting to swell from early arthritis that shouldn't happen to a man in his forties. If Thomas took better care of himself, would these things show up? If he didn't drink so much? If he rested more, took care of himself? If he was happier?

No, Thomas wasn't going to give up, but it might kill him.

CHAPTER 6

ASSAD SAT ACROSS the table from the new recruits the prophet in Chicago had sent him. These were children. One of them had lost a brother in the little Nashville raid when the SEALs took over their compound. Several others knew brothers-in-arms who had been arrested, which was a blessing. The work would continue from the prison, if it was God's will they should spend time there. A congregation of the believers was growing every day inside prison. They had everything they wanted, including conjugal visits with their 'wives' since most of the guards couldn't keep them straight.

The only thing Assad had missed out on was the sex with the Nashville girls. He would have wanted to do that. Smoke some pot, have sex with an infidel, make her think she should be the vessel for his seed, try to impregnate her, and then sell her to the sheikh's supporters in Oregon, or, better yet, in Iraq or Syria. She'd be bearing what they called an "anchor baby," an automatic ticket to obtaining a U.S. Passport.

The American girls were so gullible. When his friend had written him about the deflowered infidels, one he'd deflowered himself, his dick got hard. He wanted a young American virgin; a blonde, or some fiery red-head, like the whores in Pakistan. Except these American women would be blonde or red all over. He wondered what that would look like, red or yellow hair between their creamy thighs, not black, like he'd seen in the pictures of girls at home. Black hair wasn't sexy. He wanted them young and ripe, before they had any hair at all, or blonde. That was his dream every night before bedtime.

God is good. If it is your will, I shall serve the prophet in this way.

He rubbed himself at the excitement of it all. Underneath his woolen robe, his hardness was growing.

"So we have been given an order from the Mosque in the Great White City. We will follow the warrior SEALs, but you must keep your distance. We will lure them with their women."

These boys grinned, obviously delighted to play with Legos or new comic books. They had no idea what they were getting into or that some of them would be sacrificed. Their parents were being held hostage in most cases, convinced the White City Mosque could run interference and they'd be purchasing protection at home in exchange for them giving up their precious boys. Only the most cunning would ever make it out alive. Those would turn into 'coyotes,' as the sheikh in Chicago was fond of calling them. It was their version of the Mexican coyotes who brought people across the border, he was a bringer of boys to further the cause.

"You will tell us, Assad, how we do this," the handsome one questioned. His dark eyes and shiny curled eyebrows made him resemble a young attractive girl. No doubt, his ass could be mistaken for a young girl's to some of the older followers and the ones who had spent much time in prison. Or so it was said.

"Sayid, you beautiful boy, they will fall in love with you and your eyes. You will speak to them in soft, hushed tones. You will read them Rumi."

Several of the boys reacted. Rumi was not allowed in the schools.

"Yes, you will read about being their beloved." Assad continued. "You will massage their breasts," and he demonstrated it with a smattering of "Ohhs" from the boys. "And tell them you are devoted to them forever and forever. You will kiss them, this way." He grabbed Sayid and forced his tongue down the young boy's throat. Sayid protested and finally broke away, wiping his lips with the back of his sleeve as the others laughed.

"To some girls, if you feel them up, down there," he pointed to between his legs, "they have to marry you.

Some churches actually preach that."

"It is forbidden to read Rumi, my teacher, or to buy the books," one of the other boys said. "So how do we obtain such poems of love you speak of?"

"Amazon. I have an account. I am a Prime Member! Free shipping, two days!"

The boys were impressed and let him know their approval.

"I will arrange to give each of you a book. You will memorize the lines to one poem, and then we will burn them so you don't have to tell your parents you have touched something unclean, these books of Rumi."

While the boys were smiling and agreeing amongst themselves, Assad was thinking how very few of them would ever see or hear or be able to talk to their parents again. They were cannon fodder, but useful and essential cannon fodder.

"When you find the woman you want—and you will find many beautiful women in Nashville, unlike Chicago—when you find one, she must be yellow or red-haired. Promise me you will not fall for a dark-haired or tan-skinned woman, okay? You will all take proper wives of that color, and you will love them and make their bellies ripe with your seed, but these women here in America, before you have done the good work to cleanse yourself to be worthy of a good Syrian bride, these women must be of the pink-skinned type with yellow or red hair."

He never questioned why the sheikh was so hell-bent on the blondes or red-heads. He knew lots of the ladies here made their hair that color. He figured he was on a need-to-know basis, and whatever the reason was, it wasn't going to be made public anytime soon.

"So when do we start?"

"You have already started, my pupils. You are here. I will show you a few places we've been told about. We have some targets, but you will be out and around the city of Nashville, scoping out other targets. When the day comes, and we have some months to do this, we must be ready to act swiftly."

He showed them the office of the contractor who had built the structures on the compound's land. The man himself was a target. His deflowered daughter was another, and as he showed them her picture, there were appreciative nods and stares from the boys, most of them salivating.

He showed the picture of the young Afghani woman, Alfari. "This woman was the young bride of our former sheikh. She was kidnapped and separated from him and then had to endure seeing her husband gunned down in front of her eyes."

The protests were loud.

"But she allowed the infidels to take her. She went willingly with them. She must be made an example of.

Her parents were told the price was not paid, so they have given consent for a mercy killing. That will bring them the protection they seek and will right the terrible wrong done to them and their family's future."

"The U.S. government will allow a mercy killing, teacher?" one of the boys asked.

"Yes. They practically condone it. You'll see. Whomever does this deed will be praised at home and will probably never serve any jail time here."

He observed their faces as this sunk in to most of them. A couple of the boys apparently didn't believe him.

"They are afraid of us, boys. They do not want to stand up and cause a war on their own soil, even though it has already started. They're too stupid to know it."

Then he showed them the pictures of the compound where the SEALs had been bunking. "We have lots of targets here. We will watch them and their every move. We will go where they go, and we will make notes on who they speak with. Those people will also become our targets."

He leaned back and allowed them to examine the drone pictures of the SEAL camp. They also poured over the overhead pictures of the Riverbend Maximum Security prison, and one boy recognized someone standing in the yard he'd known back home.

"They think they have destroyed us. They do not

know that we know so much about them or that re-placements have arrived. Three of you will enter this high school in Nashville, sponsored by the church we have been working with." Assad showed them pictures of the red and brown brick Oberon High School with the American flag flying outside its doors. "You are to observe and make friends, look like normal teenagers. Find out where they go, what they are thinking, and find the ones who wish to have drugs. Those weak ones will usher you into their commune. "You'll find fast friends, especially if they can make some money off of the drugs you provide them. For these teenagers, the more money they make, the happier they are. You will never tell them about this group, never tell them anything about your country or your beliefs. Or your family. You will make it all up. You will learn that story just like you learn the Rumi poem. You will appear to be a brown-skinned teenager, but you will have the heart of a warrior, and your good deeds will live on for a thousand years. God is good!"

"God is good!" the group answered.

CHAPTER 7

JAMESON WAS HAPPY to see the SEALs enter High-way to Heaven just as his first set was getting under way. There were more of them tonight. None of them brought women, something that wasn't lost on the normal female population in the club; but there were so many women a dozen or two found their way over to sit with the SEALs, which didn't begin to make a dent in his cheering section.

Instead of going back to his dressing room, he left his guitar on stage, told the band to take a longer than normal break, grabbed his rum and coke, and stepped off the stage at the right, winding his way between ladies until he found the men in baseball caps.

"Howdy. Glad to see you back. They didn't charge you anything at the door, did they?"

"Yeah, they did." The tall medic shrugged. "That's how you get paid, right?"

"Yes, but Reed, that's the owner, told me he'd let you

guys in." He looked up at Reed who was busy at the bar pouring drinks. Thomas raised his glass. Jameson waved him over, and the man ambled over to the crowd. "This here is my best friend, Thomas Becker. He's my opening act, which you missed, sadly. He's a helluva songwriter and taught me everything he knows."

Thomas wrinkled his brow and puckered his lips. "He's a liar."

"Thomas, these are SEALs from San Diego."

"So what are y'all doing in Nashville?"

"We came for the music," one of them barked.

"Long way from San Diego," Thomas insisted. "How long are you here for?"

"Going home tomorrow, actually," answered the medic. Jameson liked the tall SEAL with the kind eyes. He and several other SEALs close to him were not interested in the girls who had brought chairs and were chatting the other SEALs up.

The club was packed. Jameson scanned for evidence that the producers were in the house, but didn't find them. "So tell me, if I can ask, how did you become a SEAL?" he asked Cooper.

"My parents were farmers in Nebraska. I thought about farming. Lots of guys go into it. My dad and granddad wanted me to. My sister and her husband lived in the same house as my folks and my granddad. I don't know, I just saw myself doin' something else."

"Like getting shot at?" Jameson's interest was piqued.

Cooper looked at him a long while. "It's sort of a calling, Jameson. Just something you find you have to do."

"But why?"

"Why do you do this?" the Puerto Rican SEAL asked.

"The money. I want to sing professionally, you know, get a record deal, be a star."

"And so you're doing that. How does it feel?" Cooper asked him.

Thomas had overheard them. "Yeah, Jameson, how does it feel?" Then he launched into song, "To be on your own. Like a rolling stone."

The laughter wasn't comfortable. In fact, it pissed him off. Thomas was becoming someone he didn't want to hang around anymore.

"I love what I do. I can't see myself doing anything else." Jameson knew it was a lie as soon as the words left his mouth.

"We do, too," Cooper returned.

One of the newcomers leaned forward. "Son, we're honored to defend this great country of ours from its enemies. That's what gets us all juiced up. And like Coop just told you, it's a calling."

Jameson sat back and thought about the man's comments.

"This here's our LPO, Kyle Lansdowne," said Cooper. "He kind of leads us when we listen."

Several of the SEALs laughed as Jameson and Kyle shook hands.

"I guess I defend this country against lousy music, then." Jameson was having fun with them now.

"There you go," added Thomas. "How long you boys been in?"

"Some of us have been in over ten years. A couple of the young ones came right out of high school."

Scanning the group of SEALs, he understood an unspoken comradery between them. He noted the way they looked him in the eye and answered questions so directly.

After they talked a few minutes longer, he heard the band begin warming up on stage and took that as his cue. He had spent his whole time chatting with the SEALs and hadn't lined anyone up to go home with. Perhaps that was for the best, he thought.

"Thomas, make sure Reed knows their tab is on me. And tell him he's an asshole for charging them anything to come in here. They're heroes in my book, and heroes don't pay."

"Will do, boss. Go make me proud," Thomas said, as he slapped him on the back.

More people had entered the Highway. The second set was going to have the biggest audience he'd ever played to. He picked up his guitar just as a barmaid handed him another rum and coke, which he sipped, and then toasted the room. The crowd loved it.

"Okay, this is for the heroes in the room. We got any heroes here tonight?" He put his hand over his eyes to tone down the lights. A couple of drunks from the audience stood up and were pulled down. None of the SEALs stood. He watched Cooper and Kyle shake their heads. He knew it would be a mistake to call them out. "Well, I happen to think we are honored with some very special heroes here tonight. This here's for you."

His All-American theme song was what he played at 4-H auction events and sometimes small local fairs. The crowd knew it well and started to clap and cheer. Thomas sat up straight and saluted him, since it was the song Thomas had written some ten years ago that he was sure would make a hit record.

The rest of the set went smoothly. Thomas appeared to be enjoying the conversation with a couple of the SEALs, and he envied the man. In fact—and this had never happened before—he wished he was down there talking to them and Thomas was up on stage. For the first time in many months, he was not seeking someone from the front row. He knew there would be the opportunity if he stayed behind to sign the small posters Reed had made of the week-long gig. But that wasn't what he was focused on.

He finished the set, came back for the encore, and

played two more songs, including his 'come fuck me song' that Thomas turned around for, giving him another salute.

"Thank you for spending your hard-earned money to come hear my music," was his final word to the audience. As an afterthought, he pointed to the SEALs. "Don't you boys go anywhere. I'm gonna be right back."

He wasn't sure what it was he wanted to say to them, but he put his guitar in the base, picked up his black bag in the dressing room, drank what was left of his now-warm rum and coke, and headed out to the theater.

He stood amongst them. Cooper was the tallest. "It's been a real pleasure and honor that you came to my show tonight. If I get this record deal, and I'm thinkin' I will, I'd like to dedicate it to you boys."

Cooper shook his head. "Totally not necessary. We have all the recognition we want or deserve. You're a helluva singer and songwriter. I think you really got something there."

Several of the other SEALs came over and shook his hand. Jameson noticed that they all laid their money down on the tables, ignoring the tab that was supposed to be on him. They were quietly making their way out toward the doorway when he heard one of the men say, "Hey, Red. How's that ankle?"

Her face pinkened as she addressed the group, not sure who had called her out. "I'm fine. I told you guys last night I'm fine."

"That you are, sweetheart," the same SEAL answered back. "Here I just met the love of my life, and I gotta leave her behind." Several of the others patted him on the back as they began filing outside.

Kyle, their leader, was last to shake Jameson's hand. "You get tired of picking this guitar and playing for whiskey, you come out and visit us some time. We'll show you some clubs you could do well in. 'Course, it's not Nashville. And the girls, well they're pretty, but not as pretty as this little one here," he nodded to the redhead. She blushed.

Jameson accepted a card from Kyle. "Thanks, man. Appreciate that. If I ever venture out that way, I'll look you up."

"You do that. We'll go do man things, jump out of airplanes an' shit—pardon me, ma'am." Kyle bent to acknowledge her. "Until then, you break a leg, or don't they say that in the music business?"

"Nah. We just say, 'Give 'em hell.'"

"That's what they tell us, too, and that's pretty much what we do, I guess," Kyle answered with his wide smile and affable manner. Jameson liked the man instantly. He was a leader without being obnoxious or pushy. He was a fresh drink of water to some of the types he'd had to listen to and be around. In the music industry, a smile might not really be a smile, a handshake not really an agreement between two honorable men, in a town where you didn't really know who to trust and who was stealing from you, where robbery of the soul was as commonplace as hookups at bars and as certain as the bevy of women only too willing to stoke the fires of a young man's ego.

Kyle made an unremarkable exit and was just gone. That left him standing behind with the redhead. Thomas had said his goodbyes earlier and headed over to the bar.

He focused on the lady standing by his side. She smelled wonderful, looked soft and warm as a country kitchen. She was very pretty, without much makeup, which he preferred, and as he studied her blue-green eyes, he was affected by the gentle way about her that was soothing, not asking or expecting too much of him.

The crowd was becoming drunker, boisterous belly laughs piercing the smoke-filled space, and he didn't like the fact that Arlen wasn't anywhere around. Remembering the trouble that had occurred last night made him more than a little concerned.

"I'd offer you a drink, but I'm needing to leave this crowd. You wanna come back to my place for a bit?" It was the first time he'd actually asked a girl to his room. Her eyes angled down, hesitating, so he decided to let her off easy, if that's what she wanted. "Oh, it's all right, darlin', no offense. I didn't mean anything by it. Maybe I'll see you around another time."

Her face came to pretty attention. "No, that wasn't it. I'd be happy to have a drink with you at your place."

He gave her the room number and the name of the hotel.

BACK AT THE hotel, Jameson took the card from his wallet and flicked it back and forth between his fingers a few times. He didn't believe in coincidence. There was some reason he was meant to meet these men tonight. Kicking off his cowboy boots, he opened a fresh bottled water without opening the minibar. A part of him just wanted a shower and a deep sleep. If she took too long coming over, he would be asleep in his clothes. He sat in the reading chair at the corner, staring at his TV, but without turning it on, listening to the words playing around in his head.

The gentle knock on the door jolted him awake. He had fallen asleep for just a few seconds. In his stocking feet, he turned the handle and found the redhead standing in front of him.

"Hi, Jameson."

"Come on in," he said, like he always did when he saw a pretty woman standing there.

She sat on the edge of the bed, which was different. She still had the strap of her purse over her shoulder, which made him wonder if she was planning on bolting or staying.

"You want something?"

"Something strong."

That nabbed his interest, so he chuckled. "Okay. Needing an ounce of courage, are we?"

"Yes."

"Really?" he turned in her direction to make sure it was the same girl he'd thought he'd let in. He opened the minibar. "We got vodka, orange juice. I got Jim Beam, little bottles of crummy wine, some beer, or what's—"

"I'll have the Jim Beam."

"Okay, I'll join you. You wanna wait here while I go for some ice?"

"Only if you want it. I'm fine."

He started to walk toward the bathroom to fetch a couple of glasses when she stopped him. "Just give me the Jim Beam." She stood, extending her arm.

He did. She screwed the top off, toasted her tiny bottle to his tiny bottle, and downed the whole thing in one long gulp. She closed her eyes and licked her lips, and as he watched her, he could feel how the liquor was flowing down her spine. She resumed her seat on the bed. He was left standing without having touched his liquor, he was so stunned.

"I need to take your temperature, darlin'. Am I *that* bad?"

"No, don't be silly."

"Maybe you misunderstood my intentions, and if I

need to apologize, I'm game. You mind telling me what's so hard about being here that you have to take a drink before you can talk or anything? Are you okay?"

"I'm fine." She kicked off her shoes, which made him feel a little bit better.

"Come, sit. Here." She patted the bed next to her.

He took a seat in the reading chair several feet away from her and waited. He wasn't sure he was going to like what was coming next.

"Jameson, you obviously don't remember me."

Jameson's full attention was on the little lady now. "I'm sorry, but, no, I—"

"I know. Too many women, too many shows, and too many towns. How could you keep them all straight?"

"I think I'd remember you. So what you're saying is that you and I—"

"Yes. Several times. At my parent's ranch, too, in North Carolina."

The fog began to clear. "That was a long time—" He stopped and tried to remember her, and did. But she was a blonde then. And yes, she was the one from Charlotte. "Lizzie?"

She nodded, examining her fingers entwined in her lap. She wasn't smiling when she looked up at him. "Good. I'm glad at least you remember."

"Of course I remember. One of the best weeks of my life. Your dad and mom were so nice to me."

She examined her hands again. "Both gone now, sorry to say."

He came over to her and kneeled in front, placing his hands on her upper arms and rubbed her gently. "I'm so sorry, honey. It's the red hair. I never would have recognized you if you hadn't told me."

He took her hands in his and pulled her fingers to his mouth, kissing them. She eyed him carefully as if thinking about bolting. He dropped her hands, but stayed kneeling in front of her.

"How've you been, honey?"

"I've been well. My folks passing has left me enough to have a little house in the country. I sold the horse ranch."

"Oh, I'm sorry to hear that."

"Well, I'm not. I mean, it reminded me too much of them. I just couldn't keep it."

"I'm so glad you looked me up. I always wondered whatever happened to you. Thought maybe I'd see you sometime on the road."

"No, Jameson. I don't do that. I'm not into taking numbers and waiting in line, even though it's feeling a little like that now."

"Wait a minute, honey, I asked *you* here tonight, remember?"

"Well, maybe you're gonna reconsider this after what I have to tell you. I just wanted a quiet place to be able to have this conversation."

"What is it, honey?" His hand lay on top of hers still folded in her lap. His thumb rubbed her forefinger. Then he brought her palm up to his lips and kissed her tenderly again, her familiar soft scent opening up something he'd buried.

"You have a daughter, Jameson."

He stood, the shock of it sending him reeling.

"How is that possible?"

She angled her head and squinted, staring up at him. "Really? You don't understand how it works?"

"Well, I thought we—" He began to pace, rubbing the back of his neck. The room seemed extra warm, and he could smell faint traces of cigarette smoke that weren't supposed to be in a non-smoking room. When he didn't wake up from his dream, he stopped in front of her. "How old is she?"

"She's three. She was conceived that week we were at the ranch, I'm pretty sure." At last a smile formed on her pretty face. "She's lovely, Jameson. She looks just like you. She has your eyes."

"Why didn't you come find me?"

"I'm just doing good being here now, talking to you. I was prepared to spend the rest of my life and never tell you."

"Why?"

"Oh, I guess I didn't want to know that you might

not be happy about it. I still don't know how you feel about it. I'm not asking for anything. I just wanted you to know. I'm not asking you to marry me or meet her or take any responsibility for her. My life has been fine as a single mother, and having her has been the greatest joy of my life, honest. It's all good."

"I wish you had told me. It wasn't fair you had to go through all that alone."

She inhaled deep and then spewed it out. "I'm not lying; it was hard. Nearly broke my father's heart, too, when I told him I wasn't going to see you and make any claims. He thought you'd want to know. I think that's probably why I'm here tonight. Whatever happens, Jameson, I'm glad I had her. She is the love of my life. She doesn't have to be a part of yours. That's not why I'm here. I just wanted you to know."

She stood up to go.

"Wait. You've just come here to tell me this? Now you want to leave?"

"Of course. I never came to rekindle anything we really didn't have in the first place, Jameson."

"We spent a wonderful week together, Lizzie. It was special for me." He walked over to her and pulled her into his arms. "Lizzie, I was crazy about you. Do you know I wrote songs about you?"

She accepted his embrace, but didn't intensify it. "I've wondered about that. Anyway, thanks for being such a good sport."

"Good sport? Are you kidding? I'm a father."

"But not if you don't want to be."

"Not a question of what I want. I *am* a father." He pulled back, placing his fingers under her chin and lifting her lips to his, and whispered to her softly, "Thank you. I'm so sorry I wasn't there." Their lips touched, and as they rubbed against each other, he remembered the spark that had become that beautiful bonfire between them.

"My folks were wonderful. They loved her, right up until the day they died. They were killed in a car accident two years ago. It's taken me this long to adjust, get my affairs in order, and then I knew I had to face this. I wasn't sure I'd be strong enough to see you disappointed or angry with me."

"How could I ever be disappointed, Lizzie? Just not possible."

He would have made moves on her, perhaps try to encourage her to stay, but he didn't want to manipulate her. She'd already suffered with the consequences of his poor decisions earlier. He certainly didn't trust himself now. But he knew he didn't want her to walk out of his life again.

"Stay. Stay with me tonight, Lizzie. No sex. I'm not asking that. Just let me hold you? Please?"

In the awkward silence, after he'd asked her for the third time, she agreed.

She left her underwear on, and he left his red, white, and blue boxers on. He slipped under the covers in the darkness, and she came to him, fitting perfectly in his arms. He kissed her forehead and felt the tears flow down onto his shoulder when she laid her head against him. His thigh touched hers in a natural movement she didn't pull away from. Unforced, his arms encircling her, holding her shaking body, he was at peace with the world and suddenly grounded like he'd never been before.

It had been a day of firsts and was continuing to be so. Everything about today had been unexpected. And now he was a father.

Would he be able to stretch his heart to include her, as well as the woman in his arms who had borne him that child? He knew his life would never be the same.

CHAPTER 8

S HE WOKE UP alone in a strange-smelling bed, knowing it wasn't hers. And then she remembered. Morning sunlight streaked through the window to her right. The chair in the corner was in shadows, and someone was sitting there in a pair of red, white, and blue boxers, bare chested.

Jameson.

She didn't move a muscle, just let the view of him wash over her, felt her heart beat faster. He was in repose, with one leg crossed over his other knee, left hand playing an imaginary keyboard on the arm of the over-stuffed chair. His right bent at the elbow, long fingers moving slowly back and forth across his lips, his eyes calculating, searching something he saw or something inside him. She wasn't sure he could tell she'd opened her eyes, but she deliciously stole the seconds watching him in the early morning light.

She hoped he was thinking about her, but realized he

probably was considering all the information she'd given him. He'd been a gentleman last night. He never once made a gesture to slide his fingers somewhere dangerous or kiss her anywhere but on her forehead or on her cheek. But his arms around her waist told her something else about the man. She'd been right to fall for him so hard. Not smart in the way it happened, but watching him now and hearing his reaction last night to her story about Charlotte, she knew that her instincts had been correct. He was an honorable man, and it wasn't his fault he hadn't been a part of Charlotte's life.

He was a protector. He'd been that way when they'd made love so many times over the course of those golden days. He'd been a careful lover, attentive, and she allowed herself the luxury of feeling fully consumed by him, nearly to the point of tears half the times they'd been together. The beauty and the mastery in the way he made her feel stirred, healing everything hurt and incomplete in her soul. Mating with him—and that's what it was—not making love or having sex, it was a mating ritual, a religious experience.

After he had left and went back on the road, she was seriously hoping to follow the circuit he was traveling and show up at some future venue when she found out she was pregnant. That changed everything. It changed her whole life.

There wasn't a day that went by that she didn't think

of him. As she brushed Charlotte's angel-spun hair, braided it into tiny braids no bigger than the size of her shoelaces, when she tucked her under her arm and read a story to her, or when the little one stared up into her eyes, she saw him there. It was only a matter of time before she was old enough to ask, *where's my daddy?*

Lizzie figured she could always say he'd gone away, just like her father had, before Charlotte was old enough to remember him. That brought tears to her eyes. She was happy her father was able to meet his granddaughter before he passed. At the same time, she was sad that she would forever miss the relationship only a loving man like her father could give Charlotte. This meeting was for her, after all. This was to give Charlotte the chance at a man in her life that she could call father, if he wanted that. But if he didn't, well, then Lizzie would spare her that uncertainty and the pain of being unwanted.

There was no other way to do it but to show up. *Take a number* as she'd told him last night. She'd arranged for her Nashville friend to babysit Charlotte overnight. Her friend's toddler was nearly the same age. Kendra's husband had been killed overseas, and so the two of them spent time together, raising girls without fathers or husbands. They were good support to each other during the dark, lonely times.

She moved her legs and stretched her arms up over her head, noting when Jameson sat erect and took notice.

He dropped his hand from his lips to the chair, seeming to take a minute to adjust to the sight of her again, and then stood slowly.

"You sleep okay?" he asked her.

She arched back and did another stretch. This time the sheet fell back from her white lace bra, and she quickly covered it up, returning a shy grin.

"I'll go make some coffee," he whispered, walking around the foot of the bed in his boxers. The tent in his shorts was hard to miss.

"Jameson, come here for a second first."

"I'll just be a second," he whispered as he disappeared into the kitchenette. She listened to the water running and the gurgling sounds sending a fresh caffeine scent she loved even as a child.

He sat on the bed and handed her the ivory crockery mug filled with the brown steamy liquid. "I don't have any cream. Sorry. Just the powdered stuff, and I remember—"

He stopped himself and gazed off through the lighted window. She had propped herself up in the bed, her knees bent, clutching the mug. With one hand, she allowed two fingers to trace down his upper arm from his shoulder to his elbow. He tilted his head to watch her touch him and then took stock of her expression. Their eyes made the connection they always had, but he didn't act on the impulse she could see was there.

He sighed and once again took a sip of coffee and stared out the window.

"Tell me, Jameson. I've had three years to get used to the day I'd see you again. And I'm just as unsure as the first time I thought about it."

He nodded his agreement, clutching the mug in both his hands, his long tanned back barely visible in the early morning shadows. She found a way to touch his back without spilling her coffee and gained his attention back.

"Thank you for being a gentleman, Jameson."

His smile was lopsided. "Well, I appreciate that. Maybe you can tell me what we're doing here."

She waited until he looked her in the eyes again. "I think the room's beginning to get warm."

"Well, I agree with you there."

"Should we talk or—" She smiled instead of finishing her sentence.

His attention was revved to full alert. He licked his lips, set down his coffee cup, and slid under the sheets next to her. She nearly spilled her mug. "I think you better take this," she said as she held it out to him.

He set her coffee on the floor, so close she heard the clinking of the ceramic. He climbed on top of her body as she pulled her knees to the side and, leaning on his elbows, let his fingers lace through her hair. One thumb dragged along her lower lip. With complete focus, he inserted his thumb into her mouth. His chest rose with his inhale, just before he bent down, his thumbs caressing her cheeks on both sides as he took his kiss at last. His fingers gently cradled her head. They fell into the warm intensity and familiarity of what their combined chemistry had always been, and was building again. The sights and smells of the room, the talks from last night, even her years as a single mother, all floated away. She was focused on her need for this man. It was basic, like breathing, something she'd held back and hadn't allowed herself to own. Releasing those portions of her soul felt so good, to be lost in the arms of someone who transported her to the heavenly delights as a real woman, not a plaything. Again, her emotions got the better of her. When he came up for air and looked into her eyes, he carefully rubbed the tears away.

As if reading every breath she took, absorbing every expression on her face, he let his fingers draw down to her panties. The smell of her arousal was unmistakable, seeming to drive him wild. He urgently pulled them off her, spread her nether lips with his thumbs again, and kissed her there, sucking and biting her nub as she arched backward from the pulsating pleasure he brought her. The sight of his light brown hair between her legs sent off a warm tickling sensation, a delicate feather was lightly brushing up her spine. Her skin was warmed all over, her nipples engorged and hard, craving his touch. Her ears buzzed. Her breasts ached, bulging under the confines of the lacy undergarment. His lovemaking started slow, then gained gradual speed as he rose up again and searched her face, intent on the way she bit her lip. His fingers pinched her nub, and he drank from her arousal. Her moan was all for him.

He lowered his mouth again, finding her opening, laving her while her rocking pelvis performed the dance for his hot tongue he inserted deep.

Suddenly, she could take no more and pulled under his arms as if she could lift him, bringing him up on top of her, begging for his cock.

"Please, I need you inside me."

He slipped down his boxers with ease, and her fingers clutched his muscled butt cheeks as she pulled him hard into her, eliciting a resonant moan from his massive chest, his arms bracing his shoulders. She melted beneath him as he arched, rocking forward and back over her lower body, spreading her knees wider, and begging for his thrusting penetration.

Briefly separating, he found a condom in the nightstand easily within reach and began to sheath himself, but she pushed his hands away and finished, squeezing his cock and letting her hand wrap around him tight. She led him to her opening, her fingers still forming a ring at the base of his stem, as he slowly eased his stiffness inside her, feeling every half inch at a time. She'd closed her eyes at the sheer power of their joining, feeling that place with her fingers as his body entered hers, getting lost in it.

He whispered in her ear, "Lizzie, look at me. I want to see how it makes you feel."

Her muscles went into lockdown, and he groaned. "I remember this," he whispered again. "And something else," he said, as he kissed her ear, sucked on her earlobe, and found her bud with his other hand. Pressing it between his thumb and forefinger, he shattered her.

She began to shudder and shake, rockets going off behind her eyes, the delicate hairs under her ears washed in his long, languid kisses. When she pressed her neck to his mouth, she felt the sharpness of his teeth as he bit his way down to the tops of her shoulders. He lifted one knee up, holding the back of her thigh with one massive hand and slipping her lower leg over his shoulder. Having better access, he slowly added his forefinger to his own girth inside her, at the same time sliding his middle finger up the end of her sex, following the trail of her engorged lips to tap her sensitive anus. He did not penetrate her there, but rubbed her moisture all around her little flower in a ring. Her internal organs pulled at him again, and she pressed his buttocks, digging her nails into his flesh and gripping hard so that his granite shaft produced the dull ache against her cervix. She held him tight as her body milked him, not allowing him to move.

He began a long moan as his hips pivoted upward,

his thrusts becoming more urgent, burying himself deep inside her, each plunge deeper still, until he held himself against her vibrating walls, catching the tail end of her orgasm, and riding her body until she caught her breath and began to calm.

A thin line of sweat drained down the small of his back. His forehead was covered with beads of perspiration. She blew into his face. He closed his eyes and accepted the gift of her breath. When he opened his eyes, they stared into each other's souls.

How could she have even considered not seeing this man again? She reached down, pulling the sheets up over both of them. He collapsed, still inside her, and, within seconds, began a deep sleep.

She didn't want to wake him, loving the heaviness of his body as he rested against her, making it hard to breathe. The difficulty of her rising and falling chest was a labor of love. His warm body covered her completely, including one of his arms clutching the fingers of her hand out to the side. She loved that his sleeping form demanded she still be his.

Maybe that's what she'd been afraid of. What if she'd had to say no? What if he wasn't the man she thought of as a magical memory? What if he had transformed into some other kind of predatory creature commanding her submission?

She knew she would have resisted him. But relief

flooded her body. She could trust her feelings, her yearning for him all these years. Her instincts had been spot on. And just like magic, he had brought the one most perfect and precious thing into her life, Charlotte.

It was unfair to expect too much, but in the luxury of his arms and surrounded by the scent of him making her drunk with joy, she inhaled, grabbing all she could gather, and hoped these memories, too, didn't have to be relegated to some distant archive she'd bring out only when she couldn't hold it back any longer.

All that she could hope for had happened. He wanted to be Charlotte's father and had accepted his paternity, as she dared to believe he would. And she hoped there would be room for her in there, too. Her mind wanted to embrace the vision they could be a family. But even if they weren't meant to be a family, he would be Charlotte's daddy.

And that was way more of a future than she ever thought possible. She'd take it one day at a time. Whatever happened, she'd accept it with her full heart.

CHAPTER 9

"WE ARE GOING on a field trip this evening. We will gather after evening prayers. Light refreshment will be provided, and then when we come back, we shall feast before turning in for bed. You will do an hour of study before we dine, before our field trip. Wear your western clothes, but wear the ones you've had washed, not the new ones."

Assad opened the Rumi book and began reading.

'With the Beloved's water of life,
No illness remains.
In the Beloved's rose garden of union,
No thorn remains.
They say there is a window from one heart to another,
How can there be a window where no wall remains?'

Most the boys had a confused look on their faces. "Sweet cherubs, you have no idea how the pleasures of a woman can turn your heart. Understand, some of you have been sent by parents who know you might become martyred. 'How can this be?' you say. The woman gives to you the baby you send off to war."

One of the boys sitting toward the front, his best and brightest pupil, turned around behind him. "Answer the teacher," he demanded of the crowd. He was the one they all feared. Assad knew he would make a great leader because he did not care for feelings, which helped with some of the difficult decisions.

"So, Ari, you tell them then." Assad nodded to the pupil.

"I have felt the calling of a woman. What the poem is saying is that as your loins increase, as you swell and ache to join, it is a false sense of duty and loyalty."

"Exactly! Ari has stated it perfectly. How can a window exist where there are no walls? In other words, they have merged, become one. This is a very dangerous concept." He held his finger to the air, stressing the point. "There is only one calling. There is only one love greater than all others; it transcends the limits of the flesh."

Assad walked over to the side, looking out over the green rolling hills of the farm they'd rented. The land in Tennessee was beautiful. Lush and greenish gold this time of year. It was as if Mother Earth, as the hippies in America called it, was ripe with abundance, distracting her people from their true calling. It would be easy to fall into the beauty of this land, to lie in her arms and explore her valleys like he would a lover.

"The temptations are greater here. But so is the opportunity. The Americans are weak people. They trust everybody. They don't like to 'make waves' as they say it." Assad knew they enjoyed when he spoke English idioms. His eyes rolled as he pretended to be a surfer on a surfboard somewhere in the ocean he'd never seen.

The students chuckled, similar to what he'd remembered as a schoolboy at his mother's skirts. Again, his breath was taken away at the purity of their thoughts in face of the hell he was going to ask them to create. They'd walk into the blast furnace of their cause with a smile on their faces, willingly. And Assad knew that every time they would do this the Americans would be afraid. They grew weaker with each new bold confrontation. He wanted them not to feel safe in their land of milk and honey, wanted them to think everything was falling apart, as it would one day. They blamed their own police, everyone in charge. Soon, they'd be running in the streets like the band of thieves they really were. Selfish, beaten down by a soft belly and a lifestyle that didn't prepare them for the blood that was coming.

"The girls you will meet will want to learn things about you. You can smile and pretend to be shy. American girls love that. And let's face it," he said with a shrug, "it's true. You *will* be shy. You will see and hear things you've been told you are not allowed to see and hear. It will be difficult for you to sit next to all the pretty girls in their halter tops and skin-tight short pants. Their parents allow them to look like prostitutes. Even the nice girls do it. Some of them are embarrassed by what they wear, yet they do it anyway."

The boys whispered amongst themselves, adjusting their prayer robes.

"So you pretend you are a shy boy from Syria. That there was no future for you there and you must come to the States to live with relatives. You will read them these love poems." He held up the little book. "And they will fall all over you for them."

The consensus of agreement was there. The school uniforms had been purchased; not real uniforms, but jeans and American Keds, sweatshirts, plain tee shirts, and even black hoodies for each boy to help them fit in. They weren't allowed logos at the school, so Fatima and the ladies had been careful to take along one of the mothers who volunteered at the school and was their liaison.

"Teacher, I wish to ask a question."

"Okay. What's up? Please stand and face me when you ask a question."

Young Sami scrambled to stand. "If it is wrong to read Rumi back home, why isn't it wrong to read Rumi here? And wasn't Rumi a believer? My sister told me—"

"Your sister? Your sister reads Rumi?"

"No, Teacher, but she told me Rumi lived nearly a thousand years ago. At one time, it was considered scholarly to read Rumi."

Assad held up his book. "You think this is scholarly?"

Let the lover be disgraceful, crazy,
Absentminded. Someone sober
Will worry about things going badly.
Let the lover be.

"You think it is responsible to let yourself go like that? To fall into the clutches of a woman who lets you fuck her, over and over again, until you are crazy? That is the stuff of whores, Sami. That is an addiction to the flesh. You must be addicted to God and to his people. There is no greater good."

"But we are to break the teachings here. You are instructing us to do something we could not do at home."

"Correct. Because these girls you'll be meeting are not worthy of the air they breathe. In that sense, Sami, you are allowed to cull them from the population of this land so we can claim it for our kingdom. That makes all the difference."

CHAPTER 10

JAMESON RODE BEHIND Lizzie's car outside the Nashville city limits until they came to a modest neighborhood of smaller homes on average-sized lots. It was a blue collar neighborhood with an assortment of toys in the front yards like an occasional motorcycle or older RV. The yards were fenced and generally kept simple, but nice. He imagined that most of the people who lived here were at work.

She stopped in front of a yellow home with off-white trim. A pink plastic trike with pink and purple streamers and yellow foot pedals was parked just inside the fencing. A pile of shoes, adult sizes and a few child's sizes, including crocs, were scattered over the doorstep. Lizzie rang the doorbell, and he heard "Mommy" from behind the door. The window beside the front door was covered by narrow mini blinds with several of the slats twisted, leaving gaps. Jameson saw a pair of brown eyes examine him from one of those gaps.

When the door opened, Jameson came face-to-face with a little angel. Her nearly white-blonde hair was floating out of braids that had ceased to hold the hair at bay. But her eyes were unmistakable. They were his eyes. The same color of aqua, clear and almost backlit. She quickly refocused on her mother.

"Mommy," she shouted as she leaned forward, nearly leaping from a young woman's arms into Lizzie's. She buried her head in Lizzie's neck and gave her a hug, all the while staring up at him.

Lizzie's friend eyed Jameson like he was a rare and lethal bug, her arms now crossed. At her side, a toddler of about Charlotte's age, with chocolate brown eyes and a coffee and cream complexion, gripped her thigh and waited.

"Kendra, this is Jameson Daniels. Jameson, this is my best friend, Kendra."

Lizzie's friend didn't offer her hand when Jameson stuck his out. She scowled at Lizzie. "You comin' or goin?" she asked as she ignored Jameson without any acknowledgement. He wasn't used to the frosty reception; but then, under the circumstances, he gave her the benefit of the doubt.

"I'll be taking her and heading back to North Carolina tonight. Thanks, Kendra," Lizzie answered her.

"Sure thing. I'll go gather her stuff. Come on in, but our house rules say take your shoes—holy cow, those are nice boots!" She allowed a sneak of admiration to filter up to him, but then quickly covered it up. "But you still need to take them off, cowboy."

"No problem." Jameson sat on the porch bench and began following her instructions. Lizzie slipped her shoes off easily and stepped onto hardwood floors in her bare feet and red painted toes. Jameson placed his boots next to hers and walked in his stockinged feet to the small living room.

"Come on, Charlotte. Let's find your bags, okay?" Kendra begged, holding out her hands for the toddler.

"I want Mommy to come."

"Oh, soon you're gonna have Mommy all to yourself. Help me pick up your dolls and things, and then we can visit with Mommy's friend, afterwards, okay?" She shot a pointed look at Lizzie. Charlotte eyed him carefully again as she was led away to gather her things.

Lizzie took Jameson's hand, and they sat side-by-side on the only couch in the living room. A large toy box in the corner had a lid in the shape of a princess castle. Jameson had never spent much time around children, even less around little girls not yet school age. He squirmed in his seat, crossing and uncrossing his legs.

"You nervous?" she asked him.

"Depends on what you're gonna tell her."

"Well, anything I tell Charlotte, she'll forget. Or is it Kendra you're more nervous about?"

"Well, to tell you the truth, neither one of them appears to have warmed to me at all."

Lizzie giggled. "I remember that about you. Always worrying about things. You need time to let it sink in, Jameson. We've been here, what, all of one or two minutes?"

"Honey, I'm way out of practice. You forget where I hang out most of the time."

"Yup. Bars and hotel rooms. Not sure either one of them picked up on that, so just relax and enjoy the tension."

She gave him a sweet smile, but Jameson wished he could find a really good reason to bolt. He had been the one to insist he meet his daughter, and he wondered now if he should have taken more time to adjust, since it had been less than twenty-four hours since he'd learned about her.

"Don't mind Kendra. She's protective, and I do the same for her. We watch each other's backs, sort of like you and Thomas."

Before he could object, Charlotte came running into the room in a pink cape that sparkled in the sunlight, wearing a princess crown. Without warning, she jumped into his lap and leaned against his chest as if she'd done it many times before. In her right hand, she held a monster dress-up doll with big tits, wearing red high heels, jamming it up into his face, nearly smashing his nose.

"What's this?" he asked, as he peeled the doll from her chubby fingers and held it out in front of him. "Holy cow. That's a strange lookin' thing, isn't it? What's her name?"

Lizzie and Kendra laughed.

The answer wasn't something he could make out.

"They make these monsters sort of variation on Barbies, except this one is a zombie. See the bloodshot eyes and dark circles under there?" Lizzie was having a ball with his shock.

"And the green face. My mother would have burned this thing after sticking pins in it and decapitating it," Jameson said, handing the doll back to Charlotte. Lizzie was frowning. "Sorry, Charlotte honey, but I gotta say that's one ugly woman."

Charlotte leaned back and did a stare-down. "She's supposed to be creepy, silly. Don't you *know* anything?"

Lizzie giggled.

"How old did you say she was?" he asked her.

"Only three, going on eighteen."

"That's a fact," he said, nodding to the top of Charlotte's head.

Kendra brought them both a sweet tea with lots of ice. Jameson was grateful for the distraction. Charlotte wiggled her way off his lap and onto the floor, yanking her sequined cape behind her. In the process, her crown fell off, but she left it alone.

Jameson leaned over to Lizzie. "She's beautiful, dar-lin'. But shouldn't she be playing with princess dolls and such, not green monsters?"

"Who never die. I can see you didn't like mystery as a kid."

"No, ma'am. I can't sleep if I watch one of those vampire movies. Talk about creepy; now that's creepy."

Lizzie leaned against him, wrapping her left arm under his and squeezing herself into him. Less than twenty-four hours ago, he was messing around with his guitar, thinking about his care-free single life, getting ready to take a quick nap before heading over to the club. Now, everything had changed. He felt ill-equipped to care for a daughter or a wife. Being on the road performing wasn't for a married man who wanted to stay married. He hadn't known anyone who'd been able to do it success-fully.

Twenty-four hours ago, he was not thinking of any-thing permanent, certainly not marriage and raising a family. It was still something he wasn't sure he was ready to do.

"So you're taking off tonight then?" he asked her, while still focused on Charlotte.

"Don't worry, Jameson. You don't owe me anything. I set out to do what I intended to do. You've met her. Now the ball is in your court. We'll be fine, either way."

He wasn't sure what he should say. He was used to

being confident, assured. He was used to going at his pace, which was easy and slow, until some beautiful and exciting creature with ten times the need he did would drag him into an exciting liaison and love the night away. And then it would start all over the next day.

But for the first time, he didn't know what to say or what to do. If he left right now, Charlotte would never remember him. But he'd forever feel like a heel, and although he and Lizzie weren't married, every woman he slept with would make him feel like a cheater. And it wasn't Lizzie alone he'd be cheating on. It would be Charlotte, as well.

Suddenly, his idyllic life didn't seem so idyllic any longer. He had important decisions to make, decisions that would affect two other people's lives. There was no question that Charlotte was his daughter, but was he ready to be her father?

CHAPTER 11

WITH THE GIG at Highway to Heaven over, Reed brought in the girl group he'd bumped Thomas for. Jameson had heard nothing from the A&R guy or the producer who had initially expressed interest in his new song. He began writing a couple of other songs and considered going down to visit Lizzie, but was waiting to hear about a possible week-long gig in California, close enough to San Diego that he could hang out with the SEALs. He rented a tiny efficiency apartment in Nashville while he waited. He called Lizzie every day.

The California trip finally fell through.

"Fuck it, Jameson. We should just go there and check things out. Spend a couple of weeks in the sun, get out of this rain, see how it goes, and then come back. If something breaks, you can always come right back."

It hadn't taken much for Thomas to convince him, so they arranged the trip. Jameson called Kyle, who was excited to hear from him and offered a place to stay, cautioning him to stay away from the bachelor SEALs.

Thomas was handed a gig that was too good to pass up. He'd be touring in the Pacific Northwest for a whole month. Jameson was happy for his old friend. He decided to ask Lizzie to go with him.

"No, Jameson. I don't think it's a good idea."

"And why not?"

"Charlotte has her routine here. She's in preschool. She doesn't know you."

"Well, how the hell's she supposed to get to know me if I never see her? I'm not moving to North Carolina."

"Well, I'm not moving to Nashville or San Diego."

"Let's just take a trial run, a trip out there, and we can explore the area together. Have you ever been?"

"Never."

"Perfect, neither have I. Kyle made arrangements for us to stay at his place, and Coop offered his motorhome rigged up down at the beach. We could stay there, if you like. Right on the beach, Lizzie! Charlotte could play in the water. We could take nice walks. We'd have lots of privacy."

Lizzie's laughter was full of possibility, he thought. After several more coaxings, she relented.

They started off on a Saturday, stopping twice to overnight. Charlotte took to calling Jameson JJ, which suited him just fine.

Coop's motorhome down at the beach wasn't exactly posh accommodations, but it was rigged with a killer stereo system. He'd been told to keep his hands off of the other equipment and to leave the locked metal boxes untampered with. Jameson figured the medic had some secret stuff he didn't want to share.

The first two days they were there, several of the SEAL team came by for a timed run, then a swim, and a workout on the beach. Jameson watched them, wondering what kind of a man it took to become one of those elite warriors.

Lizzie was quiet as he studied the SEALs and then finally asked him what he thought of them.

"You know, I've never been this long from playing clubs before. Funny how, when you throw yourself out into the real world where the drink isn't flowing and the lights aren't on your face, your perspective changes."

They were sitting side by side, toes pushed into the sand.

"Could you do something like that?"

"Maybe. Been thinking about it."

He felt her stiffen. Even placing his arm around her shoulder didn't help.

They didn't talk much during the next two days. Like two ships passing in the night, he'd watch her chatting with the other wives and girlfriends at a couple of get-togethers. The SEALs valued their partying, but rarely with outsiders. Jameson knew they were beginning to consider him part of the family, and it made him proud they thought so highly of him.

Kyle invited him to swim and run with them the next morning at dawn, and Jameson said he'd be game to try. "Not much of a swimmer, but I used to run in high school."

"Swimming is no problem. Everything you need to know you can learn or we can teach you. You spend a few weeks with us, working out with us, and then we take you up to INDOC. You take the oath, and you're in."

"Whoa! In? As in the Navy?"

"Sure as shit we can nail you a guaranteed SEAL try-out, if you're not too chicken."

"Nah, I never wanted to be in the military. I'm a singer, a songwriter."

"And how's that working out for you? Where are the calls, Jameson? You got a hit record? Anyone offering to pay you a huge advance?"

"No. But—"

"Navy'll give you a signing bonus, Jameson. There's life insurance for Lizzie and the kid. If something happens to you, her college is paid for."

How the hell did I get from hanging out with these guys to thinking about life insurance and free college in the event of my demise?

"Kyle, this is a fuckin' vacation."

"Life is a vacation, my friend. Think about it. We'll meet you at your front door at zero-six-hundred."

On the way home from the party, he decided he and Lizzie needed to talk. It was obvious something was bothering her.

"I'm going to go for a run and swim early tomorrow morning. Kyle invited me."

She shrugged her shoulders. Charlotte was asleep in her car seat behind her.

After an awkward pause, she asked him the question he didn't have an answer to. "Why, Jameson? Are you thinking you want to try out for the Teams?"

"Been thinking about it."

"What about your singing career?"

"What career? I could always go back to that. But let's be honest, I'm not getting any calls, Lizzie."

"Well, for one thing, you're not back in Nashville. I wouldn't say San Diego is exactly a mecca for record producing. And where are the venues? You're not even playing anywhere."

"I'm just thinking about it. We're just working out together tomorrow, is all. Nothing to be concerned about."

She watched him with that critical eye, even though she was facing straight ahead, lights from street signs flashing over her pretty face.

"Well, I've made a decision, too. I'm going home."

He pulled over and swung around to the right so he could face her. "But why? Aren't you having a good time here? Don't you love the weather, all the new friends we're making?"

"While you're off talking to the SEALs, you mean? Jameson, you haven't been here, mentally here, the whole time."

"Yes, I have, honey."

"No. I'm not buying that crap. I thought at first you came out here to have a little vacation with me and Charlotte, but no, you came out here to meet with *them*. Charlotte and I are an afterthought." She stared at the floor. "I just realized the SEALs would always come first. That's the way they operate, and I think that's why you love those guys so much. It's a boy's club. Running around, doing all this exciting stuff like jumping out of airplanes and blowing up stuff, all the specialized training, playing with all the cool equipment and tools."

"Geez, Lizzie, how can you say that?"

"I've watched them, Jameson. Big boy scouts who never grew up."

"Who have each other's backs. Look at what they do, Lizzie."

"Just like in Nashville, your music comes first. Happy to be living the single life, different bars, different women every night—"

"That's not fair and you know it. I'm not sleeping around. Where did you get that idea?"

"Well, you're not here with us."

Jameson was fuming. He felt she had him tethered in guilt, and it didn't fit well at all. "I've been here every f—darned night and day practically, and you want more? What do you expect? You gonna suck the marrow out of my bones, too? Will that make it so you have enough of me?"

He'd mortally wounded her. He could tell she wouldn't be bouncing back anytime soon. This was way bigger than a small misunderstanding. Their irritation toward each other had been brewing for the last two days. She'd stopped initiating advances toward him in bed. It had been three days since they'd made love. No, this wasn't working out. What did she expect of him?

Now the idea of jumping out of airplanes seemed perfectly logical. He wanted to do it, just because he could.

He turned back onto the two-lane highway and then down the gravel road to the inlet and the little fishing village. Coop's 'Babemobile,' as the rest of the team called it, had seen better days. And with the tall SEAL living in it for two years before his marriage, Jameson sure hoped none of the medic's sexploits came back to haunt him. Lizzie was going through a very tender time. He was afraid to ask her anything for fear she'd snap his head off.

But hell, so was he. He didn't want to just be a sperm donor. He wanted to be a father Charlotte would look up to, a real hero. Because right now, Jameson didn't think he deserved anything, or any part of a forever.

"So when are you going home?" he finally drummed up the courage to ask.

"Tomorrow."

"I see. And when did you decide this?"

"Just now."

CHAPTER 12

LIZZIE BEGAN SAYING her farewell without tears, which was what she told herself she wanted. She held her package of sunshine. Charlotte warmed her heart, which was otherwise in terrible shape. She wouldn't say it was broken; the word she wanted to pick was disappointed. Lizzie told herself that's all it was, braced for any hint she wasn't firm with her decision, that living for three years by herself with her little bundle of joy had taught her she could do it for however long it needed to be.

But it hadn't changed Jameson's plans, she sadly had to admit. He wasn't going to become a SEAL for her and for Charlotte; in fact, they weren't even part of the equation. He was doing it for himself. And if she hitched her star to that wagon, perhaps the same thing would happen as when her parents suddenly had been gone. She could be a young widow; bringing him into Charlotte's life only to have to explain if he were killed in this dangerous lifestyle he wanted to adopt. She felt while she'd matured, as a mother and guardian for Charlotte, it would take time for Jameson to do the same, and how could he if he was gone all the time? What kind of a life would that be for them all?

Over and over again, Lizzie told herself it was for Charlotte's welfare and not her own that she was doing this. It wasn't fair to the youngster to have a man in her life, her daddy, who had priorities elsewhere. When the time came, she'd meet and fall in love with someone who could give her his whole heart. Until then, it was only prolonging the agony to try repairing something that perhaps wasn't really there in the first place. All the duct tape and barbed wire in the world could not patch that puppy. It was like nailing a ghost to the wall, putting back a feather with glue; or trying to tether a guardian angel, like the ones she loved to read about in her romance novels, with some golden string. Although, on a day like today, with the sky threatening to burst forth, she could do with a fairy godmother.

And then she smelled the golden-haired, blue-eyed angel in her arms, and all was right with the world again.

"You don't have to do this, Liz." Jameson wrapped her in his arms, and she stiffened. "Relax. Just let me hold you."

Those had been the words he'd said to her, what was it? Four, five nights ago? And she'd let him do it then and look what happened. So she pushed away from him, even though the timbre of his voice and the scent of him plucked at her heart. This would be the last time. After today, it would start to become easier, and each day thereafter, all these memories would fade.

"Jameson, I hope you find what you need. I hope you find your calling. I really do. Whether it's music or running around getting shot or worse, whatever it is you want, I hope you find it and it works for you."

"Liz—"

His hand was coming toward her face, and she veered away. "Don't. Let's just leave it where it is."

"But I don't understand why we can't give it a little more time."

"See, that's the problem, Jameson. It *was* too soon. I worried about this, and I never should have come. I thought I was stronger than this."

"You're being very strong now, but you don't have to be."

"Do you understand that I love Charlotte too much to bring someone into her life who isn't sure what he wants? Where he stands in relation to his future? To us?"

"If you want to get married, I'll do that."

"Why? What difference would that make? Is marriage some kind of magic pill you take, and voila! Everything is wonderful all of a sudden? Get married and then go off and get yourself killed, leaving us behind?"

"That's not going to happen."

"You can't guarantee that, and you know it."

"No, honestly, I can't. So you want me to stay in Nashville and pursue my music? That what you're saying?"

"No, Nashville wouldn't work, either. If I stayed by to support and watch that happen, it would only hold up until the next pretty girl forces herself into your dressing room. How long before an avid fan shows up at my doorstep saying she's pregnant with your baby? You really think I want any possibility of that happening?"

"I have no say in the matter, then?"

"If it wasn't for Charlotte, we could duke it out, hash out all the details, and maybe come to some conclusion, but this is about her, and for God's sake, I don't understand why you can't comprehend that."

Her flight was to, of all places, Charlotte, en route to Nashville, where her friend had offered her a couple of days to heal and talk through her pain and confusion. She really needed her best friend now more than ever. The flight was now being announced over the loudspeaker.

"I still have to go through security, and they're boarding my flight. Jameson, you follow your heart, your dreams. I hope you get there. I really do. And I'll follow mine, okay? Do this for me. *Find* yourself. Find someone who has the luxury of being able to wander the world with you, a great adventure, to be sure. But I'm not that person. I live in North Carolina, and I have a life I've made with Charlotte and the support system of my friends. And she's gonna be happy. Already is a happy little blessing. A little part of you, the only part of you I can have right now. The only part of you I can safely have." Her voice trailed off. She had to work to keep the waver out of it.

She wouldn't look at him. He'd put his palm on her shoulder and squeezed.

With her eyes still downturned, she added, "In time, I will be, too. I promise. Now go." She pushed him away without making eye contact, re-hoisted Charlotte on her hip, pulled out her boarding passes, and turned in the opposite direction, without glancing back.

Lizzie felt his eyes follow her all through the line, knew that he watched for some sign she'd change her mind—if she turned, he'd be encouraged by something she did. Or maybe he was already gone and it was just her imagination. Either way, she wasn't going to check. Her heart had been excised with a dull spoon.

"Bye-bye," Charlotte said, as she waved behind her to someone. The tears started to come. Charlotte giggled and continued to wave, because that's what someone else was doing on the other side of the security checkpoint line.

She handed Charlotte to the agent at the x-ray machine. "I don't want her going through this, but I will."

"Yes, ma'am. We have to do a wand check. We can do it on you both. You can hold her hand."

They barely made the plane before the doors were locked behind them. She'd had to check the stroller and one of her carry-on bags since Charlotte was a lap child on a full flight and space was limited.

She leaned back into the middle seat between two heavyset ladies who grumbled at their placement. Charlotte gave them both a stern frown when neither smiled at her. "It's okay, baby. We'll be home soon. Just try to rest, and a little later, we'll get something to eat and take a little walk down the aisle to the back. Would you like that?"

Charlotte nodded her head, and with her small forefinger, traced a tear Lizzie didn't know was showing, from just under her eye, down to the top of her lip. Lizzie gazed into eyes that sparkled like aquamarine crystals and wondered if Charlotte understood more than she was able to communicate.

"It's going to be okay, baby. Mama's okay. You take a nap."

Charlotte tucked her little face under Lizzie's chin, sighed, and—in a matter of minutes—was fast asleep.

CHAPTER 13

JAMESON WAITED UNTIL the plane took off before he left the San Diego airport. He wanted to punch something, he was so upset with himself for not running past the gate and all the guards, grabbing Lizzie, and kidnapping her back to the safety of his arms. But no, he'd been a dickwad and just watched as she made her way out of his life forever, his daughter waving good-bye like a fuckin' sad movie scene.

He climbed into his SUV and squealed the tires as he turned the corner of the parking garage. The last thing he wanted to do was show up alone and have to explain to any of his new SEAL friends what had happened. It was too early to tie one on, or maybe it wasn't. He wished Thomas was there. He'd say something either so obnoxious he could push him over or scream at him, or he'd say something that would take his breath away. Regardless, he would react. It would release some of the tension, and he'd be fixed for now.

He checked his cell phone. Thomas wouldn't be at the club yet in Seattle. He gave him a call.

"Hey, asshole."

"How's it going, Thomas?"

"What the fuck's wrong with you? This a social call, Jameson?"

"I just put Lizzie on a plane for Nashville."

"So what the fuck are you doing there in San Diego?"

"Looking for someone to get drunk with."

"This is bad. This is very bad, Jameson. I'm stuck here another three weeks, unless we get held over, and right now, it looks like that will happen. You could come up here, hang out with the band. Not like performing, but still, it would be something to do."

"Not happening. I've got some sorting out to do."

"Your funeral. You seriously considering becoming a sailor?"

"Not a sailor, a SEAL. Big difference."

"In a manner of speaking, but if you don't make it, you go out to the fleet. You're not Elvis singing to the troops and all. You'd be swabbing decks and cleaning toilets, or peeling potatoes and shit."

"Nah. I'm gonna see what it takes. I'll call back and let you know."

JAMESON, KYLE, AND Coop sat down with the Navy recruiter. Kyle told him not to trust a single hair plug on the guy's forehead and that they all lied through their teeth. Kyle helped secure an order signed by the senior staff that said he was allowed to try out for the next BUD/S class in just over a month.

It felt funny raising his right hand, taking the oath of allegiance, and receiving the sporadic clapping his three SEAL friends gave him that Thursday afternoon. Before the ink was dry, he got orders to ship off to Great Lakes, where he tested so highly they pulled him out of basic training and told him he was going to be a dentist.

"Nah, man, I'm going to try out for the Teams."

"No one makes it. I don't think they've graduated anyone in six months, son," the hardened Chief barked at him. "They don't tell the public this, but they're not adding any new SEALs. In fact, they're downsizing. Just don't want the enemy to know. I'd say dental school is much smarter, son." The Chief pressed it to Jameson's chest. "Take it, goddamn you. I'm doin' you a fuckin' favor."

Jameson called Kyle that evening and was told that was horseshit. He tore up the orders to report to dental school. The next morning he reported back to the Chief. "You guaranteed my shot, and I'm gonna take it."

The team had only been able to prepare him for a month before Indoc, so he was looking forward to testing all the training they'd shoved down his throat. Kyle and the men kicked his butt. He learned to work out with little sleep. The SEALs made him run on the beach with seventy pounds of sand in his backpack in full combat gear. They hosed him down on the beach outside the Babemobile and made him recite the Lord's Prayer so many times Jameson knew he'd be saying it in his sleep. His new friends made him carry sawed-off telephone poles by himself.

He'd pulled a groin muscle during basic, but didn't want to tell anyone when he reported for his first day of BUD/S. Sure as shit, they started doing timed runs, and his groin began to swell. When he stood up and began limping, one of the instructors pulled him out of the lineup and said, "You gonna go all medical on me or are you pregnant, because you walk like a lady who's gonna deliver triplets. I've been watching you."

"I pulled a groin muscle in basic."

"Sure you did. How many times did you get laid this week?"

"Not one, sir."

"Oh, I get it. Playing grab ass with the recruits. So you're into boys, that how it goes, sailor?"

"Nosir. Nothing wrong with me in that department."

"Did I say there was anything wrong with being gay? I'm fuckin' gay. You wanna see if I can whip your ass, sailor?"

"Nosir. I meant no disrespect."

The trainer looked him over. He picked his hands up and saw the calluses on his fingertips. "You a guitar player?"

"Yessir, I am."

"No, you're not. Your ass is mine. You might never get to play a guitar again, son. Is that gonna be okay with you?"

Jameson sighed, wondering how long the smack talk was going to hold up. "I brought my guitar, but like you said, sir, I've not had the energy to play it. But writing music helps me to relax."

"What the fuck is that? We don't write songs in the Navy. You like Frances Scott Key or something? Gonna write a new Navy SEAL song?"

"Nosir, that would be a very bad idea."

"You're damned straight." He walked around him a couple of times. "Who got you trained for this gig? You fill out well. You a swimmer?"

Jameson sighed again and examined his boots. "Nosir."

"This getting all hard on you, son? You don't like someone talking to you this way?"

"I had a soccer coach who used to talk to me like this all the time."

"That a fact? And how did you guys get along?"

"I quit the team. And I slashed all his tires."

"What the hell for?"

"He wanted me to give up the lead in the high school musical. So I quit the soccer team."

"So you're a Romeo boy. A crooner, that what you're sayin?"

"I sing and write country music, yes sir. If that's what that means."

"You get the ladies all hot and bothered is my guess. You're kinda good-looking, kid. Too good lookin' for a SEAL. We only let ugly ones pass. That's a little known fact."

"Horseshit."

"Excuse me?" The instructor leaned his concrete chest against Jameson's. "You want to tell me that again?"

"Horseshit, sir. I got friends who are SEALs, and they're damned good-looking."

"Really, and who would those friends be, or are they posers?"

"Chief Petty Officer Kyle Lansdowne, Special Operator Calvin Cooper, and a couple of others."

The instructor tried not to show it, but Jameson could tell it had left an impression on him. "So, you're hoping to be one of Kyle's boys, that right?"

"I understand it doesn't exactly work that way, but if it's possible, yes."

THAT DAY TURNED the corner for Jameson. He was

given a lighter duty than the rest of them and allowed to get a little more sleep. One by one, they learned to swim in the dirty inlet, increasing their swim and run times until most of them could nearly break records on the college level. Jameson ignored the repeated calls from Thomas and never got one from Lizzie. He focused on only one thing: not giving up.

In the end, he was one of twenty-two out of two hundred who graduated with his original class.

Kyle, Cooper, and several of the other men showed up at his Trident ceremony. He was unprepared for the fact that they'd asked Kyle Lansdowne to deliver the speech to the new graduates.

"The world's changing, gents. We'll probably have a woman graduate within these next few years. I'm not at liberty to comment about that, but the nature of warfare and the rules of engagement are changing as we sit here on this beautiful and sunny San Diego day. There are people out there," he pointed off in the distance, "who are planning right now to do us harm. Right here on American soil. That's not official Navy issue, but it's a fact. By becoming a SEAL, wearing the Trident—which I don't recommend doing, by the way, in public any-more—you are not only endangering your own life, but the lives of your wives, girlfriends, parents, brothers, and sisters.

"You don't walk in these shoes lightly. As SEALs, we

carefully train for every eventuality. And your families need to agree to be a part of this. We are all one unit. No one else understands what we do or why. We never know who ordered it or why some guy at the Head Shed decided it was a good idea to do X, Y, and Z. We don't know what political party he's a part of, because the war doesn't discriminate by political party, race, religion, or sex. Dr. Death is an equal opportunity employer. And he'll claim as many as he can get away with.

"The difference is, our families are more at risk than they ever have been. Make no mistake. You won't get out of this life before you know someone *personally* who has given his or her life to save our great country from its enemies."

Jameson was left in awe of the man he hoped to serve under.

CHAPTER 14

LIZZIE SETTLED INTO a routine over the next few months that kept her busy. Since she held a teaching credential, she was hired part-time working in the elementary school Charlotte would more than likely attend. She was hoping that by the time Charlotte was ready for kindergarten or first grade, her job would become full-time and permanent.

The time went by fast. Charlotte was very social, and at times, Lizzie had trouble keeping up with her activities and play dates. She enrolled her in gymnastics and dance classes. But there wasn't a day that went by where she didn't think of Jameson. When she didn't hear from him, she decided it was best to leave things the way they were. In time, she knew he'd come walking into Charlotte's life, probably with a wife and child of his own. She worked to make sure she was prepared for that day, when it would no doubt come.

A couple of times during the holidays and into the

spring, she traveled to Nashville and stayed with Kendra, so the girls could play and the two of them could catch up. Her Nashville friend had met an executive with one of the large hotel chains and had been able to do some traveling for minimal cost.

Kendra had received a promotion, so they decided to go out on the town, so she got a sitter from the local high school she'd used on several occasions when the two of them went out to dinner or to catch a movie. Tonight, they were going to hit the Highway to Heaven, since neither of them had been there in over six months.

When the sitter arrived, Kendra waved good-bye to the girl's mother, who had dropped her off. "Thanks for coming on such short notice, Maureen."

"No problem. I have a ton of reading to get caught up on."

Lizzie and Kendra were silent all the way over to The Highway. Lizzie thought the crowd was larger than she remembered, and it also had a younger vibe. She found Thomas at his usual perch on one of the stools at the bar in the shadows. His guitar case was down by his boots.

"I come back here after all this time, and who do I find?" She watched him struggle to lean over and take her hand.

"I been waiting for you, darlin'."

Lizzie thought he appeared even scruffier than be-fore. His jacket had a coffee stain on the breast pocket, which was slightly ripped, like it had been caught on something. His hair wasn't clean, and his face was a little sallow. She immediately picked up that Thomas wasn't his usual healthy self.

"Thomas, I want you to meet my girlfriend, Kendra."

"Nice to meet you, Thomas, is it?" Kendra was polite, but declined to shake his hand.

"Yes, ma'am," he said, as he tipped his hat to her, then removed it, and placed it on the counter. Lizzie saw the red spider veins in his cheeks and on one side of his nose.

"You playing tonight, Thomas?"

"No, ma'am. But I come prepared anyway, just in case they need the backup quarterback. I actually have a better chance to get on stage now that Jameson is gone."

Lizzy's heart raced. "Gone?"

"Oh, not dead, sweetheart." He winked at her, indicating he might be a bit drunk but his observation skills were still sharp. "Gone as in he's off to San Diego. Finishing up his qualifying. The guy actually made it through the SEAL training."

"That's awesome," said Kendra.

Lizzie wanted to learn more, but didn't want Thomas or anyone else to know that she still hadn't stopped thinking and dreaming about him. She thought she'd tucked the pain in fireproof containers in her chest, but she felt the sharp sting of unfinished business and a world of regrets.

She didn't care for being held hostage to the mystery between them, didn't want to get hit with it some day when he might just stop by and she'd have to deal with the reality that he'd moved on. "So I suppose by now he's found a nice young lady and settled down."

Thomas smirked and took a long drink of whatever was in his glass, coughing afterwards. "That's funny, missy. I guess you don't know very much about those guys. They train all the time. I mean, he was awarded his Trident, but he still has to learn how to do all this shit. They go up to Alaska, to the desert, even go to Mexico, North Africa—all over to train. I don't know how he'd have the time. But," he eyed Lizzie carefully, giving her a lopsided wolfish grin, "he's supposed to be done now."

Lizzie wasn't sure why that made her feel better, but it did.

"You know, darlin', if it's someone you want who can keep you warm at night, I'd like to apply for the job."

Lizzie wasn't sure she'd heard him correctly. If it had been anyone else, she would have let him down with a harsh reprimand involving something about him not being in her league, but because he was Thomas, dear sweet Thomas, and Jameson's old friend, she couldn't do that.

She was going to say something, when he blurted out, "Oh, hell, might as well tell you. He's coming back to Nashville. You're gonna see the posters everywhere. Old Reed has him doing a farewell tour. Seems he has all kinds of new material and might have a song or two that will be picked up."

"Really?" Lizzie asked.

"When's this happening?" asked Kendra.

"Next week. Friday, Saturday, and Sunday, right here."

"YOU GONNA COME back and see him, Lizzie?" asked Kendra, as they drove back to her house.

She wasn't sure how she felt about it. Jameson still had her phone number, and a call might have been nice if he wanted her there. In the absence of that, she wasn't convinced it would be a good idea. "I'll think about it."

They arrived at Kendra's house and woke up the babysitter. As Kendra left to drive her home, Lizzie walked inside the bedroom and found Charlotte asleep, wearing her pink sparkly cape and crown. She remembered the day she'd come running out into the living room and nearly high-jumped into Jameson's lap. She remembered other things, too: how he bent down and helped her eat her ice cream, how he walked around the house with Charlotte on his shoulders and forgot about the door jamb, catching her forehead on it and giving poor wailing Charlotte a goose egg that took nearly a week to heal.

She'd told him to find himself. *Did he?* She wondered.

Lizzie closed the bedroom door, took a shower, put on her nightgown, propped her feet up, and turned on the television. On the coffee table, a small book was open, so she leaned over and began to read some very erotic poems Maureen had left behind.

Kendra arrived back home.

"Take a look at what your sitter was reading. Honestly, these are very adult. Kind of surprising."

Kendra grabbed the book and read the title. "*Ecstasy and Love* by Rumi? Who the hell is Rumi?"

"I've never heard of him. The kids these days read all sorts of stuff. One of our teachers said her eighth grader was reading that *Fifty Shades* book. I couldn't believe it."

"But this Rumi guy was a mystic, a thirteenth-century poet from Afghanistan." Kendra wrinkled up her nose. "How the hell did she get this? I'm sure they don't teach this in the high school. This is way too adult. These pages have erotic drawings and pictures of stone carvings. Look at this!"

Kendra flipped the pages back and forth, revealing pen and ink sketches of couples in various mating rituals and photographs of stone temples with couples having sex carved into the relief.

SHARON HAMILTON

"You should call her mother," whispered Lizzie.

"I will. Wow. I'm sorry," Kendra shook her head. "I really don't like the fact that she thinks she can bring this into my house."

"I don't know. I guess I should be surprised, but I'm not."

"I'll pick one of the other girls from the babysitting pool next time. Sorry."

"It's not that big a thing."

They shared a glass of ice water and then decided to head for bed. Kendra made up the couch for Lizzie, leaving the girls asleep together in the other bedroom, and settled in for the night. Just before she turned off the lights, Lizzie fingered the Rumi pages and read several erotic poems.

When she closed her eyes, she saw Jameson's bare frame looking down on her, the feel of his kiss on her neck so real she had to open her eyes to verify he wasn't really there.

She knew, despite what she told herself, she'd be dreaming about him all night long.

CHAPTER 15

THE HIGHWAY TO Heaven was packed with the first of Jameson's three farewell concerts. He sat in his dressing room signing tee shirts, glossy pictures Reed had made up for the event, and occasionally, an arm or a thigh encased in a tight pair of jeans. It was flattering how the ladies still wanted his attention, and he had many offers for nightcaps and all-night parties. He declined them all.

Kyle, Cooper, and several of the other SEALs had come back with him for the weekend, and he had plans to show them the back streets and dark stories of the Nashville scene, sort of like they'd done for him in San Diego.

He'd been working out so much that the shirt he had planned to wear didn't fit him anymore. The definition in his shoulders and upper arms made it so he could hardly wear anything that wasn't made from stretchy material. Even his jeans were snug, his thighs packed in so tight they almost hurt.

His boots fit, though. He hadn't worn them for months.

Kyle showed his face around the doorway. "How's it hanging, Elvis?" The name that the first BUD/S instructor had called him had caught on, and he was evermore known as "Elvis, the singing SEAL." He wasn't sure how he liked it, but part of his acceptance in the community was predicated on the pranks and practical jokes that he could tolerate. Nicknames were brutal, and as nicknames went, Elvis wasn't nearly as bad as "Moron" for the Mormon kid he roomed with on one training or "Papa Smurf" for the short tight little package from New Jersey the girls called "Sugar Buns." The poor guy was barely five feet tall, and for some reason, all the six-foot-something beach volleyball players loved him, which was a constant sore subject to the taller SEALs.

"I'm good. Maybe you could help me with this. My usual shirt with all the fancy beading doesn't fit me anymore. I mean, I feel like I'm gonna pop a seam."

He held up his arms and showed Kyle how tight the back and chest were. "And look at this," he showed Kyle how little room his biceps had.

"You wanna just play in your white tee shirt? Might be more comfortable."

"No. This is a tradition. I never thought I'd have to have this damn shirt altered. It's my lucky shirt."

Kyle pulled the fabric wide at his upper torso. "You need more room here. I'd say give 'em what they want and unbutton an extra two. That'll make the room you need."

Kyle unbuttoned the shirt.

"Now I feel like Tom Jones. Only thing missing is all the gold chains," laughed Jameson.

"And the wolf patch on the chest. Don't forget that. Although I guess that's not really in anymore."

"I think Elvis did it, too," added Jameson.

"Oh yeah, I think he just shoved his shirt into his pants without buttoning it at all, especially toward the end. And then he kicked and danced around on stage with his coattails flying. Been a long time, but I saw him on TV as a child." Kyle adjusted the shirt so it hung on Jameson straight. "Perfect, cowboy. I think we're good to go."

"Okay, thanks, man."

"You need to pray? Do I need to do a laying on of hands or anything?"

"Shut the fuck up and get outta my room, you prick."

"Okay," Kyle said, feigning being careful, tiptoeing out the door. Just before he closed it behind him, he whispered, "Give 'em hell, Jameson. Let 'er rip. You're a fuckin' guitar-playing-fuckin' U.S Navy fuckin' badass SEAL."

Jameson kicked the door closed and left a boot print on the wood.

He closed his eyes and he saw Lizzie's face.

Damn.

He'd been staring at the cover of his cell phone for nearly twenty-four hours, since they hopped aboard the transport plane and landed at the Naval Air Station. He was looking for a text or a call from Lizzie, but none came. With only five minutes 'til show time, he knew it wasn't likely she'd be there. He consoled himself with the fact that perhaps he'd call later tonight or tomorrow morning and catch up, maybe invite her to one of the last two concerts. They were going to deploy in a couple of months, and up until that time, their training would be intense, without any weekend leave. So this was the last time they'd have off before then.

Grabbing his guitar, he realized he hadn't brought the rum and coke into the dressing room with him, and he'd been so busy, he'd forgotten to order one. The club body guard—a huge woman named Debbie who sported tats and wore all black leather, with bright pink lipstick matching her two-inch long, scissor-like nails—barked her question that sounded more like an order.

"You ready, sugar?"

"Yes, ma'am."

She grinned from ear to ear and sauntered over to him, not minding a bit that her enormous tits rubbed against the bare skin on his chest. Her fake eyelashes were nearly an inch long.

"Look at you, cutie. You're sweet as sugar. Man, I'd love to fuck your brains out. You game afterwards?"

In spite of himself, Jameson blushed.

She squealed with delight. "Ah, sugar, sugar, sugar, I want you to suck my pussy dry and then fuck me wet."

"That's very tempting, Debbie," he said, hoping the panic in his voice didn't show. "But I got a date," he lied.

"I don't mind. I'll bet she has a nice little ass that we could both enjoy. Or she could watch, and I'd bet she'd be so hot she'd let you fuck her from here to the moon and back. You know like that sign they have in the expensive gift shops? 'Love you to the moon and back?' That kind of a fuck."

She'd been a topless dancer in her younger years, one of those who was naturally well-endowed, and a Nashville favorite. Her string of nasty boyfriends had her taking self-defense, and when she couldn't get a job working for the Nashville Police Department because of her past drug use, she took to being Reed's enforcer, and sometimes mistress. But only if she was feeling generous. Reed practically had to beg her to go to bed with him, and he was walking behind the bar with a continual hard-on, Thomas told him.

She stood before him, poured into the size-twenty leather pants that showed every curve. "Laters, baby," she said and blew him a kiss.

Jameson took in a big gulp of air, sort of grateful for the entertainment, which was a lot wilder in his dressing room than whatever was going to happen on stage tonight.

Thank God.

He heard his name being called out, and the crowd erupted into cheers, the likes of which he'd never heard before.

The band had started their warmup late, barely breaking a sweat by the time Jameson came out on stage and began playing.

He began the set with his American Patriot song that the crowds always loved and sang along to. He gave the front-row ladies winks and the chance to become stars, leaning over the stage to give them one shot with the microphone, their friends screaming in the background.

He launched into a three-set heartbreaking series, singing about cheaters, drunks, and girls who chose somebody else. He mopped his brow with a shirt someone had thrown him and then decided to slow it down a bit.

"Okay, let's have some fun. Who here has the most tattoos?"

Instantly, the SEALs stood, ripping off their shirts, displaying Celtic crosses, barbed wire rings, naked girls, skulls, and of course, the frog prints going up their forearms. Nobody else came close.

"Honestly, I think you guys are the winners. Why don't you come up on stage? Or better yet, let's have Kyle Lansdowne come up here and show off his tats. He can be the symbolic winner."

Jameson happened to glance stage right and saw Debbie's ample ass covered in hearts of all different sizes and colors, all with a man's name written in script beneath them. And sure as shit, the bright red one on her left cheek read *Jameson*. She started to take her pants off when Kyle hopped up on stage, his eyes wide as saucers. "Holy shit," Kyle said.

"You don't know the half of it, Kyle. Unless you've got a month's supply of penicillin, you don't go near that," he whispered in Kyle's ear.

Kyle paraded like a body builder across the stage with whoops and hollers from the crowd, which was mostly made up of women.

Jameson played a few bars of *Miss America*, and Kyle flipped him the bird. Jameson then shook his finger at Debbie and pointed to her pants down around her ankles.

"Reed," he purred breathlessly into the microphone. "I think Debbie's ready for you right now, from the looks of it."

The club owner dove over the bar and came running backstage as Debbie yanked on her leather pants, which were very stubborn. She, too, gave Jameson the finger.

"Thank you, Kyle. Ladies, give it up for one of America's finest!"

Kyle hopped off the stage and returned to the rear with the other SEALs.

JAMESON GRIPPED THE microphone and gave them the warm buttery voice he knew the crowd would like. "I'm gonna sing a song I've never sung before, something I've recently written." He turned around and nodded to the band.

"These guys haven't even heard it. So it's gonna just be me."

He picked up his acoustic guitar and leaned into the stool with one leg straight and one knee bent, balancing the guitar on his thigh. The melody was simple, but one of the sweetest ones he'd written, eliciting something deep inside him. He began to unburden his soul and let the words flow out of him.

You loved the spring in Carolina
With the dogwoods all in bloom.
I couldn't pay the price of that small time life,
Second story, one room view.

He'd practiced some intricate fingering he was proud of. It made even Thomas stand up straight behind the bar as he gave Jameson the thumbs-up.

He scanned the audience, warmed by their rapt attention. He was ready for the second stanza, and as he leaned into the microphone, he noticed Lizzie walk in through the door.

He inhaled, but discovered he'd temporarily forgotten the words. Seeing Lizzie had taken his breath away. Her red dress was anything but demure, and she'd let her hair go back to blonde, just like he remembered her. She was the woman he'd loved all those years ago, and she was here again, after all that had happened between them.

"You know, folks, I liked those words so much, I'm thinking I should sing them for you again. How'd you like that?"

The crowd was into anything he was going to do on stage, and he thanked them for their support. Then he smiled at Lizzie, as if she was the only girl in the bar, and sang the words again, this time just to her.

You loved the spring in Carolina
With the dogwoods all in bloom.
I couldn't pay the price of that small time life,
Second story, one room view.

His heart melted when he saw her discreetly wipe tears away with the backs of her hands. Her girlfriend pulled her to a table, and they sat. Though she was only one out of over a thousand people waiting to hear him sing, she was the only person he focused on.

He continued with his song until the last two stanzas.

And the words you said still ring in my head
While I'm lost here in San Diego.

He stepped back from the microphone and bowed his head. Nothing ever again would be as special as singing his song of love for Lizzie in front of a room of mostly strangers. And nothing was sweeter than seeing her softly sobbing, her shoulders shaking, as she tried to stop, but couldn't. She waved off her friend, who was shooting daggers at Jameson. But he didn't care. It was one of those magical nights. He'd gotten to mess with his new LPO, the girl he loved with all his heart sitting in the distance, knowing how he felt about her; while the grunts and groans of Reed and Debbie's lovemaking punctuated the air and had the band laughing so hard they could barely play. On a scale of one to ten, this was clearly a fifteen.

A perfect night, if only she'd let him touch her, he could right the axis of her soul, kiss her tenderly, and swear to her there wasn't anyone else in the universe he'd rather be married to.

And he'd mean every word of it.

CHAPTER 16

LIZZIE'S PLANS THAT evening were to slip into the audience unnoticed, since she hadn't thought out meeting Jameson again so publicly. They'd dressed at Kendra's house, the girls playing in the background. Her friend took a look at her red dress and she whistled. "That's a statement all right. You sure you know what you're doing, Lizzie?"

"No," she laughed. Her heart was light. Some of the heaviness had dissipated as the anticipation of seeing Jameson 'made her think funny' as Kendra so often described when seeing a handsome man. She told herself it was to see him play one more time, since he was, in all likelihood, not going to become a Nashville star as he'd originally wanted. He'd chosen a career in the Navy, instead.

Many of her friends who knew him were all abuzz with his plans to become a SEAL. And this was his first time back. He'd begged off interviews, which were frowned upon by the Navy, and even Thomas said he couldn't get ahold of him. Lizzie still had his number in her phone, but never dared to call it, figuring he'd moved on, like she'd tried to.

The two girls were playing dress up again, something they did every time they were together. Lizzie knew that when the two became teenagers, their hangouts and shopping sprees would be legendary.

Their babysitter arrived, dropped off by her mother. Kendra waved to Mrs. Gunther just before the woman drove off.

"Mrs. Reeder, I need to ask you something," Cissy said, as she set down a pile of textbooks.

"Sure. What?"

"After the girls are down, would it be okay if a couple of friends of mine come over? We have some studying we need to do for our World History class. They are both straight-A students. No drinking or anything you wouldn't like. And we'll be quiet, just studying."

Kendra looked at Lizzie, who wasn't thrilled with the idea, but gave her consent. As an afterthought, she asked, "These are girls, right? Not boys."

"Well, actually, one is a boy, and one is his sister. Very quiet, respectful students. They're exchange students at our school."

That seemed to satisfy Kendra. "You okay with this?" she asked Lizzie.

"I'm not sure. Absolutely no drinking, no smoking, right? And only after the girls are down," Lizzie instructed.

"Yes, ma'am," she answered respectfully.

"You know these two well?" Kendra asked.

Cissy smiled, closing her eyes to emphasize her complete agreement. "Yes. Absolutely. They are like family to me."

Lizzie kissed Charlotte good-bye and told her to mind the babysitter, and while the toddlers were distracted with something else, the two of them slipped out of the house.

After arriving at the club, Lizzie hiked up her bra and adjusted her front so nothing intimate was showing.

"I'd give anything to be able to show off a rack like that," said Kendra. "Even breastfeeding, I didn't have tits like that."

"And I nearly drowned Charlotte on milk several times," Lizzie laughed. "I'm sure your talents lie elsewhere."

Kendra shook her head and took the lead, opening the club door where the sounds of a crowd and live guitar-playing filtered out into the night air. "I sure hope so." Her friend pointed to the room with her thumb. "Here I thought I was going to have to put in my ear plugs and look like an old unmarried spinster sister."

Lizzie drew her back into the parking lot and

touched her forearm. "Hey, it's gonna happen for you. I mean, not in a place like this, but you'll meet someone special who will make the long wait worthwhile. That's what I'm counting on."

It was what she told herself every day, but standing here, on the edges of the world Jameson inhabited, her heart beating like a kettledrum, she wasn't so sure. Her choice of the red dress belied the whole theory that she just wanted to blend in to the crowd, watch him sing, and then close the cover on that painful book forever.

Kendra sucked in her gut, gulped down a deep breath, and pulled back the door again. "Okay, let's do this."

"Let's!" Lizzie shouted behind her.

He'd already begun the set, his long lanky form perched on the grey metal stool. He looked fitter than she'd remembered him, and she had no complaints before. His husky voice resonated in her chest just as if he'd been whispering to her. The rest of the room faded away as he glanced up and saw her.

He didn't avert his gaze to keep from getting snagged by whatever non-verbal message she might have wanted to dish out. He perused her dress, licked his lips that had turned slightly up on the right, and gave her a half-smile. She felt the warmth of his eyes from clear across the room.

He spoke something about singing the same words

again, which she didn't understand, until his intense gaze hooked her heart and she heard words that had been written for her. She was sure of it. He sang without hesitation, pouring himself out to her just as if they were alone.

She felt the hot tears; the months of stuffing down her emotions, hopes, and dreams; and telling herself she was coping better each day, that she was nearly over him and soon he'd be a distant memory, just faded away. Her raw feelings for the man made her chest pound, her shallow breathing barely giving her enough energy to stand.

She wiped her face and continued to study him through watery eyes. Kendra pulled on her arm, motioning for them to sit down, and she followed along, grateful for her leadership. His warm gaze covered every movement as they sat. He continued to pour on the lovely words, making sure she understood how he felt about her, spearing her heart and leaving her quivering. Kendra leaned into her, and she brushed her off.

"I'm fine. I just never knew he could sing like that," she said, which didn't satisfy her friend one bit.

Jameson strummed the last chord, graciously nodding to the crowd, his quick glances to her raising her expectations and shattering any hope she had left of moving on and being able to forget him. It wasn't that he was a performer and he was good. It was his words and how he sang them to her. He had shown a whole room of people what was in his heart. Maybe it was unwise to dare to hope he wanted something more permanent, something she'd not allowed herself to dream or feel any longer. Could it be?

"Okay, ladies and gentlemen. There's something I gotta do right now. So, if he's willing, I'm gonna ask Thomas to come up here for a second and relieve me."

Thomas gave her a pat on the back, clearing his throat as he walked past her, and made his way up to the stage. The two men discussed something privately, and Jameson handed a folded piece of paper to him.

She saw that Thomas tried to push the paper back into Jameson's chest, but he was unsuccessful. Jameson gave a salute and handed Thomas his guitar, then her tall drink of water jumped down off the stage and headed right for her.

Chairs moved out of the way as the audience remained in hushed silence, candles flickering on the tables like stars in a clear winter sky.

Thomas began his introduction from the stage. "Jameson wrote this song as well, but he made the mistake of asking me what I thought about it, and so I made some changes. He learned his lesson with this last one." Thomas watched Jameson continue on his straight trajectory.

As he stood before her, Jameson took Lizzie's hand

and pulled her to standing position, their bodies barely touching. With hands framing her face, angling her backward, he whispered, "You don't know how many nights I dreamed about doing this. Forgive me, but I just can't help myself."

She was going to say something, at least give her consent, but he bent over farther and covered her mouth with his.

Her senses were flooded with the currents of pleasure winding around her neck, down her spine, and between her legs as he gently suckled her mouth, being careful as if she was a China doll. She inhaled and stepped to him as their kiss deepened. She placed her palm over his heart and felt how fast it was beating. Her arms slipped up his back as their tongues mated.

Thomas was trying to steal the crowd's attention, but many had stood up and begun clapping.

"Well, that's fine; yes, let's give them a round of applause. Jameson and his Lizzie. I think they're gonna be a little busy tonight, but I could be wrong."

Women in the audience were also crying. Couples hugged one another and kissed. When their kiss was over, Lizzie knew her cheeks were flushed, and it was only then that her self-consciousness rose to embarrassment—kissing him so deeply and intimately in front of so many people she didn't know. But Jameson was there, standing tall and looking as handsome as she'd ever seen him, clear-eyed and proud, focused and fully accepting.

It was a different Jameson she kissed. He went away to the Navy a raw young man with raging hormones and an ego the size of the State of Tennessee; and came back as a man who could love, show his love, and who had obviously chosen her. For the first time since she'd met him, she believed that he loved her back as intensely as she had always loved him.

"Okay, folks," Thomas began after another round of applause had erupted. "Show's over, at least that show. Now I got something special for you, but you're gonna have to forgive me because I'm not well-practiced on this song."

The audience laughed, and those that had been standing seated themselves.

Thomas picked his way through a whole stanza, giving the audience a preview of what was to come. The folded piece of paper fell to the floor as he began singing. Jameson held her in a slow dance pose and rocked her from side to side.

On a Sunday afternoon when I was feeling kinda low.
I thought I'd pay a visit to a girl I used to know.

Lizzie swayed and turned as they began a slow dance. She was having a hard time following the words, her heart was beating so loudly. She also heard Jameson humming the tune, smiling down at her.

When I stepped up on her front porch and knocked upon
*   her door,*
I was greeted by an angel's face I was sure I'd seen be-
*   fore.*

She's got my eyes,

She darted a quick look to Jameson's face and watched him softly sing the words while he swung her around to the rear of the club over by the bar.

I knew in my first glance that she was mine.
I never felt so happy,
'Cause a little girl with pigtails had my eyes.

In a darkened corner, he kissed her again. "I was a complete idiot, Lizzie. I want us to be a family. I never should have left you the first time."

Her head was swimming. The attention from the crowd and the heat between her and Jameson made her wonder if she might pass out. She couldn't speak. She pressed her palms to his chest, fingering the intricate beading on his shirt as if her life's story were recorded in the beads, smoothing over the hand-stitched work of art. Her head was trying to focus. Her mouth opened and closed, but still words would not come. His arms encircled her and pressed her close while he rocked from side to side.

Jameson nodded to Thomas on stage, who continued with the song and even managed to give him back a thumbs-up.

Jameson's chest grew large with the breath he inhaled. "Marry me, Lizzie."

Was she hearing this? Was this really happening? She closed her eyes and felt his warm cheek against hers as he whispered in her ear. "Help me to be Charlotte's daddy. Help me to be the man I want to be."

"Jameson—I just—"

"I gotta know, Lizzie. Do you love me?"

"Of course I love you. But all this—"

"You started it, sweetheart, by walking back into my life. You had no right doing that. You gave me the chance to be the man I was meant to be."

"But you just joined the Navy. You're going to be deployed."

"What? You think deployed men don't have wives and children? You think no one waits for them at home?"

"No. I didn't mean that—"

"I'm a different person, Lizzie. I grew up, became a man at last. And a man takes responsibility for his actions." He held her face again, kissing her softly on the lips. "A real man knows how to love a woman, can love a woman more than he loves life itself, Lizzie. You are that woman for me. And I promise I'll always come back to you."

She buried her face in his chest, just as Thomas received the well-deserved applause for the performance of his lifetime.

Jameson ushered her back to the table she'd shared with Kendra. As he climbed the stage, she took the hand of her friend and sighed.

"Unbelievable. I was totally not expecting this."

Kendra leaned back in her chair as Jameson began to play with the band's accompaniment. Thomas remained with him on stage.

Lizzie watched her friend shake her head. "I can't say it was unexpected. I mean, what did you think was going to happen when you wore that red dress? Poor Jameson didn't have a chance, Lizzie."

They agreed that Lizzie would stay for Jameson's second show and Kendra would go home to relieve the babysitter.

"Are you happy, Lizzie?"

"Yes."

"Well, tell your face. You look like you stepped in front of a huge semi."

"It's just so fast."

Kendra folded her arms over each other. "Really? You honestly can't tell me you ever stopped loving him. And it has nothing to do with Charlotte, either. You've loved him for over three years."

"You're right," Lizzie admitted. "Thanks, Kendra. I'll stop by in the morning, and if you're game, we'll all go out to breakfast."

"Don't make promises you can't keep. I don't work tomorrow, so you go have a good time. The girls and I will be fine." She leaned over and kissed her cheek. "Love you, sweetie."

"Love you, too, Kendra. Thanks."

LIZZIE WANTED TO go back to Jameson's dressing room at the break, but didn't want to interfere with whatever he and Thomas were discussing. Jameson gave her a wave and blew a kiss, holding up his ten fingers. She blew him back a kiss and put her right hand over her heart.

It had been a perfect night. She was looking forward to their reunion later on, alone.

NEAR THE END of the second set, Lizzie got a text from Kendra. She noticed she'd had her ringer turned off and had missed two calls from her as well. What she read in the text message blew up her world.

The girls are gone, Lizzie. The babysitter, too. They're gone!

CHAPTER 17

W HEN JAMESON AND Lizzie arrived at Kendra's
house, two police cruisers and an unmarked
vehicle were pulled in front and in the driveway, so
Jameson parked a block away. He grabbed her hand,
leading her carefully, racing toward the front door until
they were stopped by two uniformed policemen.

"Our daughter is one of the victims," Jameson reported to them. He was still catching his breath, but felt
Lizzie jump at the use of the word "victim."

"I'll escort you in," answered one officer. He led the
way, Jameson and Lizzie following right behind him.

Once they were inside the living room, Kendra stood
up, her face was ashen, streaked with tears, deep lines in
her forehead, and her eyes puffy. "God, Lizzie. I'm so
sorry about this."

Lizzie collapsed into her arms. The two women consoled each other while Jameson introduced himself to
another officer inside the house.

"You think the babysitter could have taken them some place on her own, like on an errand?" the officer asked.

Kendra broke free of the embrace and spoke up. "No. I know the family. She would never do something like this."

"What about her friends, Kendra?" asked Lizzie.

"Friends? She wasn't alone then?" asked the officer.

"Well, she asked permission to have a couple of her classmates from school come over to study after the girls were asleep. We reluctantly agreed."

"I'm going to need the information on the friends, in addition to your sitter. That's Cissy Gunther?"

"Yes. Look, I called her home a few minutes ago, and that's why I called you guys. Her mother didn't know anything about this, and she didn't have the car. So they would have had to leave in one of her friend's cars, if her friends were even here."

Kendra glanced at the policeman and at the plain-clothed detective who was on his cell phone. Jameson knew there was something she was hiding.

"You told him about this?" the policeman pointed to the detective on the phone.

"Yes. I think they're scouring for a yearbook, for a picture of her. The principal is coming over in a few minutes, too." She examined her slippered feet. "Lizzie, they're treating this as if it's a ransom for hire. Expecting there will be demands for cash for the girls. They're bringing in equipment to listen for a ransom call."

Jameson didn't believe that theory. Lizzie had told him about the book of poetry and the possibility that exchange students had been at the house. He knew it was no coincidence and had a sick feeling in the pit of his stomach.

He'd called Kyle, letting him know what was happening. Kyle and several other SEALs were on their way over to help with a possible search. What they needed was a break, someone who had an idea about who was responsible, or knew *something* about these people. Otherwise, it was like finding a needle in a haystack and would be a huge waste of everyone's time. Not that it would stop them from trying.

The plain-clothed officer informed them he'd notified the FBI, who had asked to be briefed.

"So you're not convinced this is a ransom situation, that right?" Jameson asked the older gentleman.

"Well, I can't ask them to jump in here without something more credible. It will eat up man-hours and such. We get a phone call or someone knows something about this babysitter, we go from there. But we're prepared for every eventuality."

The high school principal was ushered in by the same officer who accompanied Jameson and Lizzie.

"God, I'm so sorry. I brought the files the police

asked me to bring. I'm afraid I can't be of much help."

Jameson needed to ask a question of the detective. "You asked all the neighbors yet? Maybe they saw something?"

"Yes, we have two on it right now. It's taking a while because most everyone is asleep, even with all the activity going on here."

"Mr. Daniels, we're detaining a guy who says he's your boss outside. I can't let him in here, but do you want to go speak with him? He's more than a little persistent." The young uniform grinned. "If you know what I mean."

"That would be Kyle," Jameson said. "I'll be right back."

On his way out the door, he watched as the principal handed the plain-clothed detective the file he'd brought. "These are all the exchange kids. We have them from Brazil, from France, and, this year, a batch from Syria. With the civil war going on there and all, we agreed to take in a few extra."

Jameson stopped, dead still. "You said Syria? How many from Syria?"

The principal leaned back on his heels. "Let's see, I think, six at Oberon. But a couple of the other high schools took a few, as well. We're all trying to help out."

"All high school age?"

"Yes. I believe the youngest is thirteen."

"Boys or girls, sir?" the detective wanted to know.

"Um, mostly boys. We have one girl, but the rest, as far as I know, are boys."

"She's a sister to one of them," added Kendra.

"Ah, no, ma'am. None of these students are related."

"But my sitter said he was bringing over his sister and they were all going to study together, if these are the right kids."

"Well, I'm not sure of that. In fact, if they were brother and sister, we'd place them in the same home, together. But they requested separate homes and explained it wasn't proper for her to stay with a family with unrelated boys in it. Made a big deal about that. So she's staying with the Campbells, and they have a daughter the same age."

"The Campbells?" Kendra's voice filled with panic. "As in Maureen Campbell?"

"Yes, Maureen. Is—that significant?"

Kendra faced the detective. "We found an erotic poetry book—Rumi is the author's name—left behind when Maureen babysat a few months ago. I called her mother and told her. She told me Maureen had gotten it from the exchange student they had. I didn't think to ask what country she was from."

"Ah, well, Mrs. Reeder, I doubt the presence of an erotic poetry book in the hands of a high school girl is anything like a clue or something to get us tied in knots.

Kids these days—"

Jameson had to insert himself. He knew Kyle would have some light to shed on the situation. "My friend outside? He led that raid on the compound several months ago. You know the one, where they captured some would-be terrorists and killed that radical sheikh?"

"Go get him, Jameson," ordered the detective.

"You got the Campbell's phone number?"

"Yes, I have it," Kendra answered.

JAMESON GREETED HIS new LPO, who was more serious than he'd ever seen him. "Kyle, thanks for coming. I know you guys were planning on leaving today."

"Already fixed that. So you tell me what you got. We're just here to help, *NOT* to interfere. In fact, we're not supposed to do much of anything except report and assist on U.S. soil. You know the drill. You've heard the training."

"Yeah, like the raid on the compound."

"We knew they were holding hostages, abusing them, too, and we didn't want to wait for the Feds to get their act together."

Jameson hoped he was wrong about this whole thing, but was grateful Kyle and some of the boys decided to stay back for the assist. "Well, I hope this isn't a hostage situation. These girls are only three."

"And you have a teenager, too. Don't forget that. At

least the girls know her."

"Yes. Who might or might not be in on it. I just want the girls back without coming to harm."

"Jameson, if we can obtain some good intel, we'll get 'em back for you if they're still in the area. But you have to understand, these types are never really predictable, and they're on the move constantly."

"I want you to talk to the detective who says he's trying to bring in the FBI. They're going over to the sitter's house and interviewing neighbors here. He's also talking about the girls being held for a ransom demand. It might not be terrorist-related. We don't have any evidence of that, really. Just a hunch."

"Yeah. That's a pretty good hunch, though—about the size of the Jumbo Tron in San Francisco." Kyle put his arm on Jameson's shoulder, and he took comfort from it. "Now, let's go meet your JV team. The varsity's in town."

He liked hearing that a lot.

After making the introductions, Kyle sat at Kendra's kitchen table and examined the files the principal brought.

"So you know the sitter is missing. What about the other girl, the old sitter, the one who was hosting the exchange student. You never called her back?"

"No, I didn't."

"Are they around? Maybe they know something?"

"That's what I was about to do. Let me call her." As an afterthought, she looked up at the Detective. "Okay?"

"Sure. Someone knows something. Haven't heard from my guys outside or the folks interviewing the mother, so I'm thinking we're shooting blanks."

"Estelle? This is Kendra Reeder." She paused, her forehead creasing as she listened to something disturbing on the phone. "When was the last time you saw her?" Kendra was staring back in shock at the group overhearing her conversation, her eyes wide with worry. Jameson's gut fell to the floor. He put his arms around Lizzie, who clutched him like the lifeline he was trying to be.

The detective extended his hand for the phone, wiggling his fingers. Kendra handed it to him.

"Mrs. Campbell? This is Detective Blalock from Nashville PD. When did you notice your daughter was missing?"

Jameson could hear the woman sounding frantic and learned she hadn't been missing longer than today, which relieved him.

"And how about your exchange student, um," he checked the paperwork, "Malia, is that how you pronounce it? Is she around?" He paused, waiting for the answer. "Chicago? Why would Malia go to Chicago?" After an explanation, Blalock added, "We'll be sending over some people. Not sure if we can round them up tonight, but I need you to stay home until we take a look at Malia and Maureen's room, okay?"

He sighed. "Now there're *four* girls missing. I'm gonna need additional resources. Excuse me while I go call the Bureau."

Kyle motioned to Jameson and Lizzie to follow him outside. Jameson knew he was hatching a plan.

"Listen, we need to get over to that house and find out if there's anything there that will point to where they've gone."

"Right."

"What's this about Chicago?" Lizzie asked.

"We've just learned about this other guy, this new shiekh—you know when they lose one they replace them with another one to take his place? We had one leader in the central valley in California go to prison for income tax evasion. The one before him was deported. They send replacements quick.

"But in Chicago, there's a group that worships at the White Mosque, and they are especially unfriendly individuals. Discreetly, I think we've had our eye on them, but you didn't hear it from me, okay?"

"So we go then." Jameson looked at Lizzie. "You okay with this?"

"I should stay with Kendra."

"Yes. And you can let us know if something comes up on this end. You can be our eyes and ears here.

Jameson, you, me, and the boys will head over there right now. I'm gonna need that address. Can you grab it?"

"Of course."

With the plan in place, Jameson noted the address and committed it to memory. Lizzie sent a text with Mrs. Campbell's phone number when Kendra gave it to her, and the five SEALs left for the house, luckily only ten minutes away.

CHAPTER 18

THEY ELECTED NOT to call the Campbell residence beforehand and just show up, letting Mrs. Campbell think they were with the local police. She ushered them into an upstairs room done in flowered wallpaper, which hid what Jameson knew was a dark secret. The frilly outward appearance only added to the danger he felt at hand.

A bulletin board made of covered fabric and laced with satin ribbon held pictures of dances and events, outings with friends, pets, and hunky movie stars. On the opposite wall, all by itself, was a huge poster of Jameson.

"Well, would you look at that," Fredo quipped. "We got us a fan. I'm guessing it's not the Syrian girl."

Kyle had found a picture tacked to the wall beside Malia's pillow. "I think I have something."

Jameson examined Kyle's picture of the two American girls, golden blonde hair flowing in the sunshine with their mutual Syrian friend between them in a three-way hug. In the background was a house.

"See that?"

Jameson squinted, making out what looked like a portion of a tanned, sandaled leg and a small strip of white appearing to be the bottom hem of a kaftan. He stared into his LPO's face.

"We got us a new sheikh," whispered Cooper.

"Fuck!" Jameson sat on Maureen's bed and knew the clues had just ratcheted up. The threat to Charlotte's life was more eminent.

"Jameson, you're gonna call the mother up here and ask her about this place. See if she knows it. She might not be honest with me," said Kyle.

Mrs. Campbell was in near shock, her hair falling down over her neck after trying to secure it with a clip. Her mascara had run from crying. She was holding a stiff drink and smelled like she'd had a couple already when Jameson handed her the picture.

"You recognize this?" he asked.

She squinted, working on her focus, and then recognition came across her face. "That's the Stadler's place."

"You know where it is?" asked Kyle, forgetting the rules of engagement.

"Yes, I've been there lots of times when the Stadlers lived there. But they moved to Florida about seven months ago. They tried selling the house and the little ranch. Couldn't get enough, so I believe they decided to rent it out."

Kyle and Jameson shared a look.

"It's a ranch, too? Are there outbuildings and such?"

"Oh yeah, they raised chickens, although I don't suppose they're there now. They had a small barn and a shed for the apples they picked and sold in the late summer."

"Ma'am, could you find me the address of this house, please?"

"Sure, I'll do you better. I'll give you the property flier. It has the address and a map on it. I saved a couple to send to them in Florida."

ALL OF THE SEALs had their Sig Sauers, never leaving home without them, sometimes another backup, and a KA-BAR strapped to their lower legs. No one had brought their MP5s, because they had been traveling to Tennessee to attend a concert, not go to war. Jameson heard the cursing in the background, as several felt they were under-armed and didn't care for it one bit. The only time he'd seen his SEAL buddies act nasty was when something was wrong or missing with their equipment, or they'd contracted something that Anti-Monkey Butt Powder couldn't handle.

Jameson hadn't been brought up to speed yet, so all he had was his hunting rifle, but he was a crack shot, especially at long distances.

The little house came into view as their rented van pulled slowly into a clearing just outside a good view of the front porch. On a normal day, it would look like a welcoming rural homestead. But he knew it was the prison that held his daughter.

Kyle whispered instructions again, just like they'd discussed on the short trip over. Without IEDs or little flash bombs, they'd have to coordinate their attack flawlessly, if the surveillance proved to be accurate.

Armando came back with the information. He could hear the little girls playing in one of the bedrooms downstairs, supervised by one of the sitters, and everyone seemed to be doing fine.

Jameson leaned back into a tree, closed his eyes, and nearly lost his bowels, he was so grateful. Cooper and Fredo gave him an appreciative pat on the back.

"How many inside? Can you tell?" asked Kyle.

"Didn't want to risk it, but I'm thinking I heard maybe five separate voices. They're working on something in back, a new delivery of two-by-fours and some steel and bags of concrete, but no one working at this hour."

"These fuckin' maggots. You send some of them back to the source, and then they fly the coop and set up shop somewhere else," whispered Fredo.

"Well, not this group. I don't want anyone killed if

we can help it. But if you see any of the girls in mortal danger, you have my permission to shoot. I'll get the court martial, but you'll be able to live with yourself, hear?"

"Yessir," everyone whispered in unison. Everyone readied their weapons.

They checked their timekeepers and followed Kyle's silent countdown, knowing when they were supposed to do what they'd outlined. Jameson and Jones were to go in through the window in the girls' bedroom. Armando would take the rear door with Fredo behind him, and Kyle would take the front door breach. Anyone reaching for a gun would be disabled and killed if they didn't stop. Anyone who held a hostage got a bullet to the head, plain and simple.

Like all their operations, the assault started on time with complete accuracy. The girls screamed when they heard the window shatter, running to their babysitter, but Charlotte's eyes grew wide when she realized Jameson stood before her, on his knees, ready to accept the body slam she gave him. Even the sounds of gunfire in the next rooms didn't faze her. Jameson held her close and assisted Jones in safely stowing the girls behind a mattress and box spring sitting near the outside corner. The SEALs propped the bed up with two sturdy wooden chairs and instructed the girls not to leave the area.

Jameson was carefully monitoring the emotional level

of the teenager. He could see she looked scared and sported a recent black eye. "Are you Cissy?"

"Yessir," she said sweetly. "God, I'm so glad you came."

"You hurt? Anybody hurt?"

"I'm fine, but Maureen—"

The sounds of gunfire were over, and he heard a series of "clears" and knew it was safe to begin to breathe.

"Where are Malia and Maureen?"

"Malia went off to Chicago with Maureen to prepare for the wedding." As an afterthought, she asked, "You don't think they—"

Jones interrupted, "Cops'll find them. Okay, Jameson, I'm going outside to make sure it's safe."

The tall, dark-skinned SEAL slipped through the doorway.

Jameson held the two little ones, their shaking bodies feeling cold. They were still in their nighties and were barefoot. Their feet and legs were dirty, faces smeared with what appeared to be jam, wispy hair flying up in all directions. He warmed them with his body, still aware of the sounds around him, especially outside.

"What were they going to do?"

"I'm so sorry. You her daddy?"

"Yes."

"They had these girls sold to some guy in Chicago." Her lip quivered. "I overheard them talking. The boys speak perfect English." As she watched Charlotte being embraced, she added, "I didn't know anything about this. They just showed up." She began to cry, and Jameson pulled her over next to the other two girls and huddled with them all.

The SEALs walked through the bedroom door together with a swagger he hoped to have one day.

"Jameson, why is it that whenever we find you you're surrounded by ladies?" Kyle barked. Armando and Cooper were trying not to laugh, but finally gave up.

Yeah, he knew how to charm the ladies all right. He knew how to sing a hit record and be the man on stage. All those things were good and honorable. But he was looking at the men he would die for, if need be, and they'd just saved the most precious thing in his life: Charlotte. They could swagger all they wanted, boast about their exploits, and be as obnoxious as hell, but they got the job done. For that, he would forever be grateful and not mind putting up with everything else.

CHAPTER 19

JAMESON CLUTCHED CHARLOTTE, wrapping her in his jacket. He smoothed her hair, kissed her forehead, and whispered to her over and over again how much he loved her.

She relaxed in his arms, and he was gratified to hear her begin to chatter just like the happy little girl he remembered. She was safe. His brothers had helped save her, and it now appeared she was resilient to the danger she'd just lived through. God knew, he'd be making sure she never wanted for anything the rest of her life. He would ache whenever he had to leave her, but he would always come home again to her and her mother.

Still clutching his daughter, he walked into the living room of the structure. Cooper and Fredo were stacking computers, cell phones, and piles of loose papers, throwing everything into cardboard boxes. Eight young men—children, really—sat with their backs against the wall. Four armed men lay dead on the floor.

Kyle was giving instructions to the locals by phone, directing them to bring a large van for what appeared to be quite a haul of information.

Sadly, they'd not found the sheikh, nor any of the older men, except one. He said his name was Assad, and he'd been an interpreter for American forces in Syria recently. The younger boys were zip-tied, their faces showing the shock and surprise of capture. Fredo let Assad chatter on, while the boys in front of him were restrained.

"Oh yeah?" Fredo remarked.

Assad was trying to talk his way into Fredo's good graces, something Jameson knew wasn't going to fly very long.

"You know, asshole, I'm about done with your bull-shit." Fredo picked up a wide piece of duct tape and placed it over Assad's mouth. The strip was so long that it also covered his ears.

"That's better," Fredo said. Armando pushed Assad next to his Junior Militia and used the tape to wind around the man's wrists several times.

Jameson was ready to get Charlotte home, but they waited for the emergency vehicles to arrive on the scene to take control of the prisoners and the intel.

He boarded the second seat in the van. Cissy and her other charge were helped to the rear seat, sitting securely between Coop and Fredo. Charlotte was curious at first, but then tucked her head under his chin, her fingers playing with the beads on his shirt, touching the different colors. His emotions welled up, and he began to silently sob. He didn't want to scare her, so he took deep breaths to attempt to calm himself, part of the training he'd received, but also just instinct.

His SEAL brothers let him do this in private. No one consoled him. They let him deal with his joy and his pain as the van took them back home. He now realized that for every joy in life, which was so precious and fragile, there could always be a huge source of pain.

Not today.

Today, the good guys had won. Today, they were going to live to be with the ones they loved. He was sure that Kyle and Cooper, Armando, Jones, and Fredo were missing their wives, their girlfriends, and their own children. They followed every movement he made as he hugged the miracle of his own.

When they arrived at the house, he picked Charlotte up, heading for the front stoop. She'd begun to fall asleep, which he was grateful for. Lizzie met him half way, relief on her face as she hugged them both and received a tired return hug from Charlotte. Kendra took her daughter in her arms. Mrs. Gunther wrapped her arms around her daughter, who collapsed in her mother's chest. They were led to an ambulance.

Lizzie pulled his head down. "Thank you. Thank

you. Thank you, my love."

All he could do was smile through his own tears, matching hers, and search how full his heart was, overflowing with the love of his women.

Next, Lizzie went to each of the SEALs and gave full-on, body slamming hugs and kisses, thanking them for their rescue mission. He followed along as she received embarrassed smiles from these tough guys, and saw their cheeks pink up. His beautiful Lizzie could melt the whole State of Alaska with her gracious, loving heart and warm smile. She would live with exuberance and the free spirit organically given to her from the day she was born. And he'd spend his life protecting that free spirit and making sure nothing would ever interfere with her happiness again.

One by one, people started leaving the house. Kendra transferred both girls, who were fast asleep and clutching each other, to her bedroom, instructing Jameson and Lizzie to take the other one.

"We all need to rest. I'll do the duty in the morning and bathe the girls. I'm not going to do it now, nor do I have the energy to bathe myself," her raspy voice chirped. "This has been quite a day, and I'm exhausted."

Jameson suddenly didn't feel so exhausted. He ushered his SEAL brothers outside and wished them farewell. He conversed with the police and Detective Blalock and shooed away a news crew with their satellite dish and white van. He locked the front door and saw that Blalock had put a detail out in front of the house. He was grateful for that, as well.

"You know what Charlotte told me when I gave her over to Kendra?"

"No. What, sweetheart?" He pulled her to him, wrapping his arms around her, squeezing, and feeling so grateful to be alive.

"She said, 'Mommy, can I tell you a secret?' and I said, 'sure.'"

He waited, leaning back to be able to view her pretty face in the reflection of the moonlight.

"She said, as she pointed in your direction, 'That's my daddy. And he loves me.'" Lizzie's eyes filled with tears again. "You told her."

"I don't remember any of that, honey, but I must have. It just came out, I guess."

"Well, she was listening. She heard every word. You're gonna have to remember that in the future. She has very keen ears."

"Hmmm." Her body heat began to permeate his soul. "I'm going to have to remember that." He kissed her, felt the familiar reach of her arms up over his shoulders, the way her tight nipples knotted against his chest. He squeezed her ass, lifting her up off the ground, and she wrapped her legs around his hips.

He carried her down the hallway to the little bathroom with the even smaller shower. "There's hardly any room in here," he growled as he opened the glass door and turned on the water. "So we're gonna have to conserve space as best we can. Would it be okay, honey, if I pressed you close so we both could fit in here?" He followed up his statement with a wicked grin.

"With pleasure," she said as he removed her top and her bra. She carefully unbuttoned his special shirt. "Some day, you're gonna have to tell me about this."

She carefully folded it, laying it on the stack of towels on the wicker shelf where it would be safe.

He followed right behind her into the shower and pulled her back against his torso. She held her hair up with one hand and turned to expose her neck to his lips, and he kissed her from the nape of her neck to her ear. "Love you, Lizzie," he whispered in her ear.

His fingers smoothed over her slick breasts with warm soapy water sluicing down. She moaned as he bent his knees and pulled her butt in to rest on his thighs, reaching around between her legs to feel her little bud vibrate to the ministrations of his thumb and forefinger. He found her opening, and she angled her pelvis back and forth, riding his hand.

"God, I missed you. Did you receive all the lustful dreams and dangerous shower scenes I was sending you from California just about every day?"

She giggled, removing his hand and turning, placing

it to her left breast. "So that's what it was. Here I thought I was having all those erotic dreams of you, and it was you all along coming to me. You're a sneaky one, aren't you? God, you'll never leave me alone, will you?"

His fingers found her again, and she arched back as he inserted two.

"Never. I'm going to love you all day and fuck you all night."

"Hmmm. I love the way that sounds, sailor."

The cold tile on his flesh was delicious, but not nearly as delicious as her smooth, soapy, warm flesh under his fingers. They took turns washing each other, kissing each other, rubbing against each other for as much flesh-on-flesh contact as they could manage.

Then the water turned ice cold quickly.

"Okay," she whispered. "So much for foreplay. I'm ready for the main course. How about you, Jameson?"

"Most definitely. I'm starved."

She turned off the water while he found a towel and blotted her fine body dry, kissing her here and there, wherever he thought she needed a kiss. At last, he picked her up and carried her to the bedroom, locking the door behind him.

He placed her delicately on the bed and studied her body's rise and fall to the beauty of her own rhythm.

He held her arms to the sides, threaded his fingers there, and allowed his body to find hers. Her knees were bent, her pelvis perfectly angled to accept his stiff cock in one long motion until he had completely filled her, pushing against her cervix.

"Marry me, Lizzie. Let's do this. Let's be a family. Let's give Charlotte another brother or sister. Tonight. Be my wife," he whispered as he slowly stroked her insides, her lithe body rising like the waves of the ocean, falling back into the soft bed. "I need you to be my wife more than I've needed anything else, Lizzie."

"Of course, my love. It will be so."

THE END

Sharon Hamilton

NYT and USA Today best-selling author Sharon Hamilton's award-winning Navy SEAL Brotherhood series have been a fan favorite from the day the first one was released. They've earned her the coveted Amazon author ranking of #1 in Romantic Suspense, Military Romance and Contemporary Romance categories, as well as in Gothic Romance for her Vampires of Tuscany and Guardian Angels. Her characters follow a sometimes rocky road to redemption through passion and true love.

Her Golden Vampires of Tuscany are not like any vamps you've read about before, since they don't go to ground and can walk around in the full light of the sun.

Her Guardian Angels struggle with the human charges they are sent to save, often escaping their vanilla world of Heaven for the brief human one. You won't find any of these beings in any Sunday school class.

She lives in Sonoma County, California with her husband and two Dobermans. A lifelong organic gardener, when she's not writing, she's getting *verra verra* dirty in the mud, or wandering Farmers Markets looking for new Heirloom varieties of vegetables and flowers.

She loves hearing from her fans:

sharonhamilton2001@gmail.com

Her website is:

www.authorsharonhamilton.com

Find out more about Sharon, her upcoming releases, appearances and news from her newsletter.

authorsharonhamilton.com/contact.php#mailing-list

Sharon's Blog:

sharonhamiltonauthor.blogspot.com

Facebook:

facebook.com/SharonHamiltonAuthor

Twitter:

@sharonlhamilton

Life *is one fool thing after another.*
Love *is two fool things after each other.*

The SEAL Brotherhood Series:

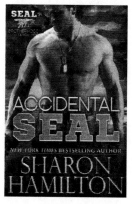

Accidental SEAL

(Book 1 in the SEAL Brotherhood Series).

Also available in eBook and audio.

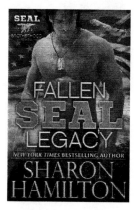

Fallen SEAL Legacy

(Book 2 of the SEAL Brotherhood).

Also available in eBook and audio.

SEAL Under Covers

(Book 3 of the SEAL Brotherhood).

Also available in eBook and audio.

SEAL The Deal

(Book 4 of the SEAL Brotherhood).

Also available in eBook and audio.

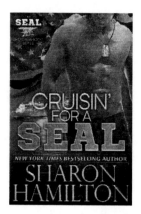

Cruisin' For A SEAL

(Book 5 of the SEAL Brotherhood).

Also available in eBook and audio.

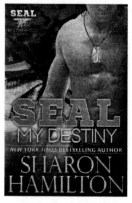

SEAL My Destiny

(Book 6 of the SEAL Brotherhood).

Also available in eBook and audio.

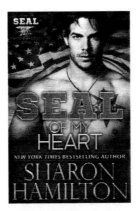

SEAL Of My Heart

(Book 7 of the SEAL Brotherhood).

Also available in eBook and audio.

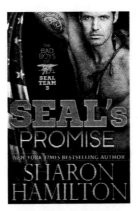

SEAL's Promise

(Book 8 of the SEAL Brotherhood).

Also available in eBook and audio.

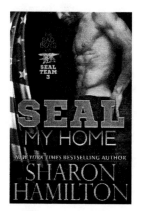

SEAL My Home

(Book 9 of the SEAL Brotherhood).

Also available in eBook and audio.

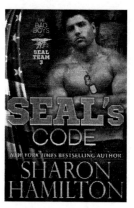

SEAL's Code

(Book 10 of the SEAL Brotherhood).

Also available in eBook and audio.

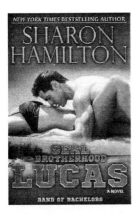

Band of Bachelors: Lucas

(Book 11 of the SEAL Brotherhood).

Also available in eBook and audio.

Bad Boys of SEAL Team 3

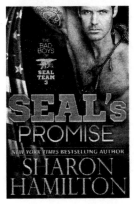

SEAL's Promise

(Book 1 of the Bad Boys of SEAL Team 3).

Also available in eBook and audio.

SEAL My Home

(Book 2 of the Bad Boys of SEAL Team 3).

Also available in eBook and audio.

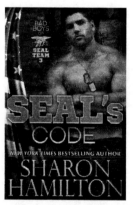

SEAL's Code

(Book 3 of the Bad Boys of SEAL Team 3).

Also available in eBook and audio.

Band of Bachelors Series

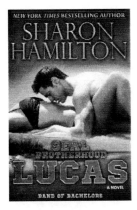

Lucas

(Book 1 of the Band of Bachelors).

Also available in eBook and audio.

True Blue SEALs Series

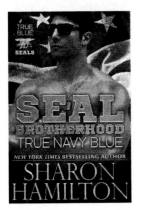

True Navy Blue

(Book 1 of the True Blue SEALs).

Also available in eBook and audio.

True Blue SEALs: Zak available in Winter 2015.

Nashville SEALs Series

Nashville SEALs

(Book 1 of the Nashville SEALs).

Also available in eBook and audio.

Other Books by Sharon Hamilton

Golden Vampires of Tuscany Series

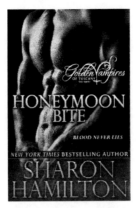

Honeymoon Bite

(Book 1 of the Golden Vampires of Tuscany).

Also available in eBook and audio.

Mortal Bite

(Book 2 of the Golden Vampires of Tuscany).

Also available in eBook and audio.

The Guardians Series

Heavenly Lover

(Book 1 of The Guardians).

Also available in eBook and audio.

Underworld Lover

(Book 2 of The Guardians).

Also available in eBook and audio.

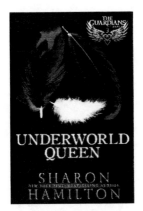

Underworld Queen

(Book 3 of The Guardians).

Also available in eBook and audio.